MRS ELSIE DRAKE is 104 years old and the sixth oldest woman in Britain. Elsie lives in London, where she enjoys learning how to use the computer, and writing very important letters to very important people about very important matters. She also loves looking after her pet hedgehog, Potsy, and making meat pies.

Elsie Drake might also be **ROBERT POPPER**, who, when he's not sending letters as a centenarian hedgehog-lover, is an award-winning TV writer, producer and bestselling author. Robert created *Friday Night Dinner*, co-created *Look Around You*, produced *Peep Show*, and has worked on such other shows as *Stath Lets Flats*, *The Inbetweeners*, and *South Park*. Under his pseudonym, Robin Cooper, he wrote the smash-hit *The Timewaster Letters* book series.

The Elsie Drake Letters
(aged 104)

Also by Robert Popper

The Timewaster Letters
Return of the Timewaster Letters
The Timewaster Diaries

The Elsie Drake Letters

(aged 104)

by Robert Popper

JOHN MURRAY

First published in Great Britain in 2024 by John Murray (Publishers)

1

Elsie Drake letters and illustrations copyright © Robert Popper 2024

A CIP catalogue record for this title is available from the British Library

Hardback ISBN 978 1 399 817 875
ebook ISBN 978 1 399 817 899

Typeset by Hewer Text UK Ltd, Edinburgh
Printed and bound in Great Britain by Clays Ltd, Elcograf S.p.A.

John Murray policy is to use papers that are natural, renewable and
recyclable products and made from wood grown in sustainable
forests. The logging and manufacturing processes are expected to
conform to the environmental regulations of the country of origin.

Carmelite House
50 Victoria Embankment
London EC4Y 0DZ

www.johnmurraypress.co.uk

John Murray Press, part of Hodder & Stoughton Limited
An Hachette UK company

The authorised representative in the EEA is Hachette Ireland, 8 Castlecourt Centre,
Castleknock Road, Castleknock, Dublin 15, D15 YF6A, Ireland

To all the amazingly kind people and companies who replied.

Author's Note

On occasion, certain names, signatures and other details have been altered or removed for the sake of privacy.

The governor of
  Pentonville Prison, ,
Caldeonian roads :
London
  london N78 TT

Elsie Drake
Granville Gardens
Lodnon

August the 2018

Dear governor of the Prison.

My name is Elsie Drake and I am 104 years of age and the sixth oldest woman in the country which is called Britin. At my time in life of 104 I have   decided to try some new things

artichoke

Cause it can get quite repetitative sitting at home with Mrs hale, she is always picking her hair, pick pick pick she is,   picking away all the time. I once saw her pick at her ear hairs,, she pulled them out in clumps.

Sir or lady, the reason i am writing is that I have never spent a night in prison before and I would very much like to, i think it would be very enjoyible. Can I stay in your prison please? I will be a model prisoner. i do not mind eating gruel or "slopping out ". But who will I share my cell with? Will they be nice ? I hop they are nice. I do not want to share my cell with someone who isnt nice.

I have never commited a crime in my life, although I did once take a bun from Mr Lannigans bakery in 1930 but i returned it after taking just one bite cause of my consience. I shall never forget that bun , I wonder where it is now? I suppose it has wrotted away.

  Please can you let me know when I can stay in your prison so i can get myself all ready.

  remember ; Elsie wants to stay in your prison.

Yours trully,

Elsie Drake

Elsie Drake (aged 104)

**HM Prison &
Probation Service**

Mrs Elsie Drake
Granville Gardens
London

31st August 2018

Dear Elsie

Thank you for your letter requesting a visit to HMP Pentonville, but before I make reference to that, can I congratulate you on reaching 104, what a fantastic age and from your letter it has clearly been a long and eventful life.

I would love to be able to welcome you here and arrange a visit. Although I am unable to offer an overnight stay in a cell, I can give you a tour of the prison over a lunchtime period, if that that suits you. I would love to be able to make it a memorable day for you, perhaps have some lunch in our staff mess – although I'm not sure we have the recipe for gruel! And you could have a look at one of our cells.

Perhaps if you or a member of your family are able to contact me, I can arrange a convenient date for a visit and if it would assist I can arrange transport to get you to and from the prison.

I look forward to hearing back from you.

Yours sincerely

**Stephen Dixey
Acting Deputy Governor
HMP Pentonville**

Mr Stephen dixey
The Acting deputy governor
  H.m.p Pentonville prison,
Caledonia n Road
London N7 8 TT

Elsie Drake
Granville Gardens
Lodnon

it is 8th September in 2018

Dear Dixey of the prison,

  I want to thank you for your lovely letter. Do you recall me ? i wrote to you cause I wanted to spend a night in one of your cells in the prison cause it is a dream of mine before I "go " to see what it is like living amongst brutes and vermin.

you said that it is nice that i have reached 104 but , sir, it is not nice. there are so many things I cannot do anymore.;

running
tether horse

I was very excited that you want to take me for lunch at you beatiful prison "Pentonville" cause I dont get much kindness anymore, Mrs hale can be a beast;; she steals my bread.

  Sir, I was very sad when you said that i cannot stay the night in the prison. Why not? I am 104 with sertification from the queen, surely that would mean i can if I want. It is the law . Anyway i have come up with a "plan " that I hope you will agree to .

I will come to your prison with my friend Bessie Bates next month . Bessie will get out her steps-ladder, which she has had since 1950 when she worked in Selbys ironmungers and needed the ladder to get iron off shelfs, I will then mount her ladder and with your permission, I will bash in the bulbs of the nearest traffic lights with a stick. You can then arrest me and i get to spend a night in the cell and fourfil my dream . Do you agree ?

But i do not want to share the cell with Bessie bates cause she screams in her sleep.

Thank you again for your kindess and i will see you on 12 of October outside the prison as that is the date Bessie comes out of hospital cause of her burnt kidney . i enclose five pounds in monies so that you do it. You are very kind .

Yours trully,

Elsie Drake

Elsie Drake (aged 104)_

Elsie Drake
Granville Gardens
Lodnon

Mr Sadiq Khan
the Mayor of London Town
the Grater london autho ority
  City hall
the Queens Walk
  London post code se1 2AA

August 9th year 20.18

Dear Mr Khan,

  My names is Elsie drake and i am 104 years of age and the sixth oldest woman in Great Britin. I am using a computor to write this letter of friendship to you.

  Mrs Hale who i live with told me that you were going to be knocking down Big ben the big clock in London town to make way for a new airport for foreign planes to land on. i said that you would never do such a thing becouse you are a sensitive soul and a lover of timepieces. Mrs hale told me to "pipe down" and then hid my bowl.

Mr Khan, sir, are you knocking down Big Ben ? Please dont. I love Big ben as it holds such memmories for me.

  one time harry Lambert took me to London town, and when the clock struck 9, he tried to kiss me and slipped on the kerbstones and broke my femur. Another time i saw a man try to jump off Big ben but thank god the police got him; he had been drinking motor oil they said.

Please let me know what is happening, I think you are narvellous.

Yours truly,

Elsie Drake

Elsie Drake (aged 104)

pS I have drawn you a picture of you and Big ben in the year of our Lorde 2018. Please can i have it back when you are dun with it.

GREATER**LONDON**AUTHORITY

Mrs Elsie Drake
Granville Gardens
London

Date: 29 August 2018

Dear Elsie

Thank you very much for your letter of friendship to the Mayor of London and for your drawing of Big Ben.

I have passed you letter on to the Mayor and he has asked me to thank you for taking the time to write.

Although City Hall does not own The Palace of Westminster, I can confirm that there are no current plans to knock down Big Ben as it is a historical and protected landmark of London and the UK.

Big Ben is home to many stories and memories to people all over the world, just as it is to you.

I do hope this letter reassures you that Big Ben will remain a feature of London for many years to come.

I enclose your drawing of Big Ben, as requested.

Thank you again for taking the time to write.

Yours sincerely

Francesca Ingram
Public Liaison Officer

Francesca ingram Mrs? miss?
Public Lisbon officer
   Works for the Mayor of London Town
      The Greater london Authority
City hall, Queens Walk
London SE12AA

Elsie Drake
Granville Gardens
Lodnon

September 3, 3rd september ,,2018

Dear miss or Mrs Ingram,

Thank you so much for your sweet leter. and kind words. I do not have much kindness in my life. Yesterday Mrs Hale told me my head was too big for my body, she said it is like a water melon. i said "no, your head is like a watermelon" "no, yours is" she said "Yours is" i said. "no, yours is" 'Yours is' 'Yours is" "no it isnt" "it is" she said. When Mrs hale went out to clean the gutter, i poured ink in her bed.

   Madam, you said that there is no currant plans to knock my beloved Big Ben down, so   does that mean there is a plan to do so some other time?

I am very scared, Will the clock fall on my head if they cut it down? it is so large might it reach me? I need some re-asurance cause I am 104 and i am frightened that the clock "Big ben " will be destroyed and the rubble thrown into the thames.

Why would you do such a thing to Ben? it is a lovly clock that keeps time to perefection.

   what has the clock done wrong?

Please can you let me know if it is being reduced to muck in a few weeks time? I am petrified of the situation. Will it cause a war? i enclose five pounds for your help.

Yours trully,

Elsie Drake

Elsie Drake (aged 104)

GREATER**LONDON**AUTHORITY

Mrs Elsie Drake
Granville Gardens
London

Date: 7 September 2018

Dear Elsie

Thank you very much for your response.

I can confirm that as Big Ben is a historical and protected landmark of London and the UK it will never be knocked down.

Big Ben is home to many stories and memories to people all over the world, just as it is to you.

I do hope this letter reassures you that Big Ben will remain a feature of London.

I am returning your £5, by recorded delivery.

Thank you again for taking the time to write.

Yours sincerely

Francesca Ingram
Public Liaison Officer

Mr Michael Roney;; chairman of
Next Shops Ltd limitted
Desford road;
   Enderby in Leicester
PostCode: LE19 4at

Elsie Drake
Granville Gardens
Lodnon

12th August is the date 2018;;;

Dear Mr Roney ,

My name is Elsie Drake and I am 104 years old and the sixth oldest woman in brittan. This is all written on a "computor". It is my first ever "computor " machine and I am enjoying it at my time of life. What is wrong with that? I am allowd to be hapy. We all are.   j;;iijhhh

   Why i am writing is i would like to work for you in Next shop clothes shop. I am looking for a new saturday job as i am getting fed up sitting here at weekends while Mrs Hale has her piano lesson. She plays very badly. Her problum is too many wrong notes. They are all wrong. I tried to tell her but she said she would hide my soap-bar again and i need my soap-bar for my dignity sir, so i just said nothing and coverd my ears while she played, but wen she went to make herself a ham sanwich i put her soap-bar in the gutter.

   Experience::: i have had shop service experience. Seventy years ago i worked in a fishmongers. I cut up all the fish and could dismantal a crab to a proficient level, well, mr Huntley was happy with my work he bought me a bun.

   Slight abcess on hip.

Mr Roney,, if i work for you, i will do my best, but i wont take any nonsense from the customers. Once two men tried to "ruffle' my hair. They were brutes but i turned the other cheek and they were soon on their way. Do you advise your employees in "Next" to turn cheeks?

I enclose £5. Please give me a Saturday job Mr roney, I would like to make myself usful to society and you are my only hope. i am 104.

Yours trully,

Elsie Drake

Elsie Drake (aged 104)

August 15, 2018

Mrs Elsie Drake
Granville Gardens
London

Dear Mrs Drake,

Thank you very much for sending your letter to our Chairman Michael Roney. The Chairman has passed your letter on to me as I am responsible for recruitment in Next shops.

I must say you have more experience than any other person that has ever enquired about working for Next. The nearest shop to your address is about 3 miles away, I'm not sure how you would plan to travel to work, it will be quite a journey in the London traffic.

Although it was a very nice thought, we cannot accept the £5 you sent Mr Roney, no one needs to pay anything to get a job at Next. I need to get this money back to you, please let me know the best way to do this, I do not want it to get lost in the post.

I'm sorry that you are not enjoying Mrs Hale's piano playing, I do hope she is improving with the lessons, I must say putting her soap in the gutter was a bit cheeky!

Please let me know how to return your money, I look forward to hearing from you.

Sincerely,

Lionel Mason
Head of HR

Lionel Mason Mr, head of hR
  Nextshops ltd. Desford Rd road
Enderby
leiceser
    LE 19 4AT;

Elsie Drake
Granville Gardens
Lodnon

August 19,2018, london

Dear Mr. mason , .

Do you remem-ber me,   I think you do cause you wrote me a very kind
letter on your "computor" . I also have a "computor" which i am using
now.   It is quite hard to press the buttons jj;'

  Thank you for being so kind sir. it is nice being kind, even animals can
be   kind. Many years ago we had a dog called " Shep" it knew nothing but
kindness,, we used to give it nice litle pats on the bottom. Shep once
found a finger in the woods but they never   found the hand.

  No i do not enjoy Mrs Hales Piano playing.   It is all the rong notes, that
is why I put her soapbar in the gutter. I am very upset that you said i am
cheeky. Mrs hale is the cheeky one;, yesterday she broke my comb.

  nits

Will you give me a job at Nextshops? i am 104 and have so much to offer
soicety.   I know how to serve the public; once a man came in and asked
for bread, we do not have any I told him.   Why should I say other-wise?

Mr Mason ,I did not get my monies back from Next shops. I sent five
pounds for their help but where is my money sir? I enclose another five
pounds .

  thank you again for being kind .

Yours trully,

Elsie Drake

Elsie Drake)aged 104)

September 10th, 2018

Mrs Elsie Drake
Granville Gardens
London

Dear Mrs Drake,

It's lovely to hear from you again.

I have enclosed all the money you have sent, there is no need to pay anything to Next if you want to work for us.

You can find jobs with Next using your computer, most people apply by visiting us on the internet at www.next.co.uk/careers. If this is not suitable for you I can arrange for someone to meet you and discuss what working at Next is like. Please let me know if you would like to do this.

I'm sorry if I upset you by saying you were cheeky, Mrs Hale is clearly the cheeky one.

I look forward to hearing from you.

Sincerely,

Lionel Mason
Head of HR

Mr Lionel mason,
Lionel
    The Head of H .R.
Next Shops LTd.
Desford road
Enderby,,   Leicester
LE19 4AT

Elsie Drake
Granville Gardens
Lodnon

Septmber 17, 2018

Dear Mr. Mason,

I want to thank you for your lovly letter that you wrote to me from "Next Shops" where you work as the Head of "H.R " but i dont know what that is. Do you do the womens clothes?

   I didnt understand when you said i can find my job on the internet cause Nicholas my great grand-son hasnt taught me the internet bit of the computor yet. We have mainly done letters and numbers and how to wash the computor with a rag if it is covered in filth .

   I would prefer to meet you   to discuss my job at "Next Shop" . I am still more or- less mobile and can get about using the bus or a "Whitsun cart ". Do you provide Whistun carts at Next Shops?

   Where do you want to meet me please?   Not in the street,   it would have to be inside where it is warm.

Thank you again for the lovly letter. I enclose five pounds monies.

Yours trully,

Elsie Drake

   Elsie Drake (age 104)

October 4th, 2018

Mrs Elsie Drake
Granville Gardens
London

Dear Mrs Drake,

Thank you so much for writing to me again, it's lovely to hear from you.

As you have not been taught the internet yet, I would like to meet you to talk about jobs in Next shops. I think it is best if you could let me have a telephone number so that we can agree the best time and place for a meeting. Please let me know a telephone number I can contact you on.

I have enclosed your £5. I look forward to hearing from you.

Sincerely,

Lionel Mason
Head of HR

Mr. Lionel Mason
t he Head of H.R
Next Shops limitted
Desford Roads
Enderby,
lecester,; LEi9 4AT

Elsie Drake
Granville Gardens
Lodnon

17th novvember,, 20i8

Dear Mr Mason,.

Thank you for your last letter you sent me You are a very kind gentleman. I hope you are hapy,, are you hapy?

I am very sorry for the delay in writing back to you. Unfortunatly Mrs Hale suffered a fall a few weeks ago and they shoved her in hospital. I visited her Tuesday last and she was in lots of horribel pain. The nurse brought her some hot soup; pea,   and when the nurse left the room i drank it all up, it was delicous.

Then when the nurse came back Mrs Hale complained that she was hungry but the nurse said "you have eaten all your soop Mrs Hale" "no i have not" she replied" "You have, look at your bowl" said the nurse. "No it was not me, i dont know who drank it" said mrs Hale. "Well you cant have any more" said the nurse . "Please" said Mrs hale.

But they did not bring her the soup.

Thank you for inviting me to your ofice. I will travel to you by coach and bus and whatnot and visit you on Friday 14t December at 3;00 in the afternoon, and I look forward to discusing my career at "Next shop"s with you. My friend Bessie Bates will acompany me. Bessie is quite a large lady and she will need a large towel . not towel i mean chair.

I will see you then, kind sir. But will you be there ? i do not want a wasted journey cause i am 104 .

yours trully,

Elsie Drake

Elsie drake (aged 104)
Ps, I enclose a drawing i did of me wearing the "Next shops" uniform . i am helping a man buy a hat for an important meeting with a governess,.

Elsie Drake working at "Nest Shops"

Elsie is helping a man customer buying a hat.

December 10th 2018

Mrs Elsie Drake
Granville Gardens
London

Dear Mrs Drake,

Thank you so much for your recent letter and thank you for the drawing of you serving a customer.

I'm sorry to hear Mrs Hale has had a fall, I hope she is getting better. I am very happy to meet you, but do not want you to go to the trouble of travelling to my office, it's quite a long journey on public transport.

Please let me know when a good time would be to visit you in London and we can arrange a location nearer to your house. I am quite busy over Christmas, January would be fine.

I look forward to hearing from you.

Sincerely,

Lionel Mason
Head of HR

Mr Lionel Mason
the Head of H.R
Next shops LtD. D esford Road
Enderby Leiceser
  LE19 4At

Elsie Drake
Granville Gardens
Lodnon

December 20,,, 2018,

Dear Mr Mason,

Thank you for your lovly letter yet again. I must thank you for the kindness you bave bestowed upon me. I am 104.

Also I want to thank you for offering to come to my house to give me my new job at "Next shops Limited', however I am very sory because I have since decided against a career in clothing shops , and I am now looking for a job as a ship-hand on a ferry.

Yours trully,,

Elsie Drake

Elsie Drake (age 104)

NO MORE LETTERS

Sir Chips kewsick
  Chairman of the Arsenal football Club
Highbury house
  75 Drayton park
Town; london N5 1BU

Elsie Drake
Granville Gardens
Lodnon

It is August the 13   2018

Dear Sir chips,

  My name is Elsie Drake and I am 104 years of age and also the sixth oldest woman in the country of britin.

When my late husband Sidney was alive (he passed away several years ago in 1950) he used to take me to watch the football at Arsenal club. We had cheese sandwiches, two buns each,, some lemonade and I sat on Sidneys knees which worked wonders in those days.

  In other words i have fond memories of footballs.

I am writing because I would like to become a special mascot for the Arsenal football team. I will come on to the grass before the men play and do a little dance in front of the crowd.   I may be 104 years old with sertification from the queen but I can still dance on command.

Music may be played i have no objection .

I have an old costume of a hare. it has dark brown fur and large ears like hares do. I will wear that. Mrs Hale doesn't like my old costume of a hare. She said that it smells rotten and was going to put in on a bomfire, and when she went outside to light one, i hid it where she will never find it. Don't worry it is safe. Sometimes Mrs Hale uses a nife to cut her own toenails.

How many football teams can say that they have a 104 year old lady as thier mascot inside a hare? it would be a talking point people will come for miles and miles to see me dance> it will be a wonderful day I will never forget it.

Please write back Sir Chips and let me have my chance to shine. I enclose £5 monies.

Yours trully,

Elsie Drake

Elsie Drake (aged 104)

Arsenal

ARSENAL FOOTBALL CLUB
HIGHBURY HOUSE
75 DRAYTON PARK
LONDON N5 1BU

24/8/2018

Dear Elsie

Thank you for your lovely letter with so many happy memories recorded — you have a wonderful memory.

I am not sure about dancing on the pitch but we will see what we can do.

With all best wishes

Chips Kerrick

Mrs. Theresa May
The Prime-minster
  of Great Britain
number 10 Downing street
London
Post code;

Elsie Drake
Granville Gardens
Lodnon

august 14st 2018

Dear Mrs. May the priminster of great Britain,

My name is Mrs Elsie Drake;; I am 104 years of age and the sixth oldest woman in the country and I have just been given a computor. I am enjoying it and can write allsorts: chair, antelop, winkles.

  I think you are narvellous and want to shake your hands for all the good fine work that you do for the country, great britin.

Mrs May, I would like to make myself usful to society and so I want to offer my services as your maid in waiting. I can clean most surfaces and cook a good shephards pie when Mrs Hale doesn't hide the meat. She is always hiding the meat so one time i hid it under my bonnet. She didn't find it. How could she? It was under my bonnet.

Will you let me work as your maid in Waiting?

  and what will I receive as a stipend? Thirty pounds? Forty ponds?

Please write back quickly . you are my only hope, I am 104 and i am sending you five pounds english pounds .

Yours trully,

Elsie Drake

Elsie Drake (aged 104)

PS, can you also please send me a nice photo-graph of your self as well please ?

1O DOWNING STREET
LONDON SW1A 2AA
www.gov.uk/Number10

From The Direct Communications Unit

17 August 2018

Dear Mrs Drake

I am writing on behalf of the Prime Minister to thank you for your letter of 14 August.

Your correspondence is receiving attention.

Yours sincerely

Correspondence Officer

1O DOWNING STREET
LONDON SW1A 2AA
www.gov.uk/Number10

From the Direct Communications Unit

31 August 2018

Mrs Elsie Drake
Granville Gardens
London

Dear Mrs Drake

I am writing on behalf of the Prime Minister to thank you for your letter of
14 August 2018 and the £5 note.

The Prime Minister appreciates the time you have taken to get in touch.

Further to the response you may have already received from this Office. I hope that
you will appreciate that it would not be appropriate for this Office to process
monies, so I am returning your £5 note to you. I am delighted to enclose a copy of
the Prime Minister's official photograph, as requested.

Thank you, once again, for writing to the Prime Minister.

Yours sincerely

Correspondence Officer

The Rt Hon Theresa May MP
Prime Minister

Mrs. Theresa   may
the Primeminster of Great Britin
Number 10 Downing streets
London,;, sW 1a 2AA

Elsie Drake
Granville Gardens
Lodnon

new month: "September " 3rd, 2018

Dear the Prime minister,

I wrote to you on "august 14st of this year" but i am a littel upset with your letters that you sent back, mam.

i wanted to be your "Maid in waiting", so i can cook you pies and wash your nesessaries,, but the lady or man that wrote to me from your "correrrespondence unit:" just sent me   five pounds monies. Does that mean that is five pounds in loo of my working for you as your maid in waiting ?

Is it in loo? If it is in loo, then when do I start at number ten Downing street as your maid in Waiting? do i come next week? and do i bring a bumpkin?,

I am very good at scrubbing. Once i scrubbed an entire scullery with Bessie Bates. It was filthy, we found a pile of dead mice ,dead flies and maggots that came up to our bosom. Poor bessie caught a terible infection and they had to lance twelve boils from her body. but then she got a fever and started biting everything in her sight; tables, the floor, she even bit a light bulb that was plugged in and her arms caught fire cause of the electric currant.

I enclose five pounds and i am 104 and i need to know if i should be getting the bus to you next week to start scrubbing for you. can you tell me mam?

Are sandwiches provided?

Yours trully,

Elsie Drake

Elsie Drake (aged 104:)

1O DOWNING STREET
LONDON SW1A 2AA
www.gov.uk/Number10

From the Direct Communications Unit

13 September 2018

Mrs Elsie Drake
Granville Gardens
London

Dear Mrs Drake

I am writing on behalf of the Prime Minister to thank you for your letter of 3 September 2018 and the £5 note you sent.

I am sorry to read that you were unhappy with the previous responses from this Office. Thank you again for your kind and considerate gesture, however the Prime Minister does not require a maid in waiting.

I hope that you will appreciate that it would not be appropriate for this Office to process monies, and I am returning your £5 to you again.

Thank you, once again, for writing to the Prime Minister.

Yours sincerely

Correspondence Officer

Elsie Drake
Granville Gardens
Lodnon

Mrs. Theresa May,
The British Prime Minster
Number 10,
  Downing Street
London SW1A 2AAAA

September 19th in 2018

Dear Mrs May the Prime Minster of britain,

It is Elsie Drake here again and i am 104. Thank you for your letter but I am very sad that you do not want me to be your "maid in waiting ".

  I think you are making a big mistake, mam, as I am very good at maid-in waiting. I will maid-in-wait anywhere you want, even in the toilet when you are at a conference .

To make you change your mind, i am enclosing ten pounds as a "bribe " to make you give me the job as your Maid-in waiting. I got the money out of Mrs Hale's purse when she was sleeping in her hospital bed. She is in hospital cause she fell and smacked her face on a pole outside the butchers when she was buying pork.   She is all dizzy and wont notice the money is gone.

  please buy something nice with the monies like shoes or licorice and when can I begin maid in waiting for you?

Remember;; do not tell Mrs hale about the money but there is more in her purse if you want it.

Yours trully,

Elsie Drake

Elsie Drake (aged 104)

1O DOWNING STREET
LONDON SW1A 2AA
www.gov.uk/Number10

From the Direct Communications Unit

1 October 2018

Mrs Elsie Drake
Granville Gardens
London

Dear Mrs Drake

I am writing on behalf of the Prime Minister to thank you for your further correspondence of 19 September.

As we have previously explained, this Office is unable to process monies. For this reason, I am returning your £10 to you. I would encourage you to consider whether instead you might prefer to donate this money to the charity of your choosing.

Thank you, once again, for writing.

Yours sincerely

Correspondence Officer

British Swimm-ing
3 oakwood drive
Lough-borough
Leciestershire
Post-code : Le113qF

Elsie Drake
Granville Gardens
Lodnon

Augus 19nd 2018

Dear sir /madam?

My name is Elsie Drake and I am 104 years of age and the sixth oldest woman in britin. I am writinf this letter on a fully electric computor. It is my first one ever . It does numbers and letters but i cannot find the button for "emergency 999 ". Do you know where it is?

I am writinf to you because it is my dream to do swimming in the english channel. By that I mean not just swimming in it but swimming across it from Englamd all the way to France on the other side. I will be very out of breaths when I get there but everyone cheered. it was a lovely day, I will never forget it .

cataracts removed by Dr. Bunn in 1990.

now i have some questions about it; Is the water warm ? Or is it cold? i don't much like cold water. Do I need much training or can I float all the way with the breeze?   where do I do my "toilet?" do i have to hold it in or am i allowd to expel my waste into the sea?;

I enclose 5 english pounds for help. i am 104.

Yours trully,

Elsie Drake

Elsie Drake (aged 104)

CHANNEL SWIMMING &
PILOTING FEDERATION

Mrs Elsie Drake
Granville Gardens
London

1/2/19

Dear Elsie

Some little while ago you wrote telling us that it was your dream to swim the English Channel and I apologise for the delay in replying to you.

It would take a great deal of training for you to achieve that dream but the fact that you have the ambition is an inspiration to us all.

Before we allow swimmers to make an attempt they have to prove that they have swum for at least six hours in a water temperature of 16c (61f). Swimmers also have to have a medical, signed by a doctor, declaring that they are fit to undertake such an arduous endurance venture.

You asked some questions which I can answer. The water is relatively cold, often around 16c or less, probably much the same as comes out of your cold water tap. I am afraid you cannot float all the way with the breeze so you would have to train. Most swimmers train for at least two years before making an attempt. As regards your toilet, to use your words, you are allowed to expel your waste into the sea.

With regard to your computer, it is a tribute to you that you have been able to master it to write a letter. I fear that there is no 'emergency 999' button.

I would love to help you make your dream come true and I salute you for having that dream.

Thank you for sending £5 to the CS&PF. We are proud to have you as a member of our organisation and one of the reasons for my delay in replying was so that I could send you a membership certificate for 2019 which I now enclose.

I wish you the best of luck and continuing good health to enjoy your ambitions.

Yours sincerely

Kevin Murphy
(CS&PF Sec.)

"Nothing great is easy"

Captain Matthew Webb

The Channel Swimming and Piloting Federation

Elsie Drake

is a Member of the
Channel Swimming and Piloting Federation
for 2019

Membership Number
19/031

Mr Paul Dacre
Editor of the Daily mail newpaper
nothcliffe   house
  2 Derry Stret
  London W85tT

Elsie Drake
Granville Gardens
Lodnon

The 20, of August 2018

Dear Mr Dacre,

   My name is Elsie Drake and I am 104 years old and the sixth oldest
woman in Great Britin.   I am writing to you on a new computor. You only
have to push a button to get what your heart desires.   1;;iiihg))))

Mr Dacre, even though i am 104 I would like to make myself usful to
society so I am writing to ask you for a job at your newspaper the "Daily
Mail". i have never worked in news-papers but Ive read them all my life.
Some of the things they say are shocking though arent they? I would
never allow myself to be splayed on page 3. Never Sir.

With your blessinf I would like to set up a new newspaper for you that
caters to the over 100 year olds like myself. i think it would sell very well.
The people that would buy it would be;

Me, but i would get a copy gratis I suppose.
   Other people over 100 out there
 Interested folk. Theres enough of them about!

It could be called "the Over 100s News" and we could charge 100 pence
due to the name.

My skills are; I can type as you can see, I'm punctual as long as the bus is
on time, typing, and I can use a dial phone in emergency. Please help me
be usful to society at large, sir and let me have my chance to shine.

   I enclose 5 pounds English monies to help with costs. Please reply
quickly. I am 104.

Yours trully,

Elsie Drake (aged 104)

ps I enclose a drawing of the newspaper but please can you return it
when you write back as it is my only coffee

"The Over 100s News"

100 pence

New news-paper by Elsie Drake aged 104

Inside there is:

Headlines - Britin is sinking into the sea

Sport - Golf, sand hockey

Cooking - Mince recipes

Celebritees - Peter and Ann Hand show us their bath

Sewing - How to do sewing

Free

Animal section this week - Rabbits

On Sale Now

Can you help make my dream come true and get it printed?

Elsie

Please help Elsie

The Daily Mail

Mrs Elsie Drake
Granville Gardens
London

23/08/2018

Dear Mrs Drake,

Thank you very much for your letter, and congratulations on being the sixth eldest woman in Great Britain! We greatly appreciated your suggestion for a newspaper for seniors over the age of 100, but unfortunately we are not looking to start a new paper at the moment.

However, we would love to hear more from you, and were wondering if you might be interested in writing us a letter telling us a bit more about your life. We would be fascinated to learn about the changes you have noticed throughout your lifetime, or what your childhood was like.

Please find enclosed the £5 you sent, and your plan for your newspaper.

Yours sincerely,

DM Letters Secretary

DM letters Secre-tary
   The Daily mail newspaper
Associateded newpapers Lltd
Nothcliffe house
2 Derry   Street
London ; W8 5TTT

Elsie Drake
Granville Gardens
Lodnon

August 26th.   2018 august

Dear Mrs, Letters Secretary,

I want to thank you greatfully for your charming letter from such a lovly lady, but i was a little upset that you did not want to make a newspapper for the over 100 year olds. I think it is a mistake and i am sure we would make a lot of monies.

   What would i do with a million pounds?

Thank you also for asking me to write about my life. Where would I start? I have seen so many changes;   electric ovens, radios, television, the griffith pole, planes, "the Space Races ".

Here is what i have writen for you,

My life by Elsie Drake -

I am 104 years of age now but back then i was a litle baby who did not know how much the world would change . We were terribly poor;; there was ten of us in one room. We did not wash every day like they do now, no, we would wash once every month. We would get in the nuddy and climb into a tin troff but we had no running water, we just used dirty puddle water from the road which was called "Old Puddly ". It smelt of eggs.

Thank you for your kindness and may the lord smile upon you sweetly. i enclose five Pounds for your help and I think the Daily Mail is narvellous.

Yours truly ,

Elsie Drake

Elsie Drake (aged 104

The Daily Mail

Mrs Elsie Drake
Granville Gardens
London

Thursday 30th August

Dear Elsie Drake

Many thanks for your lovely letter. I will pass that on to our Letters Editor with the rest of today's post to be considered.

I am returning your generous gift of £5, as it is not necessary, and I cannot accept it. However, the thought is very much appreciated.

Yours sincerely,

DM Letters Secretary

ELSIE IS WAITING . . .

Mr mike Coupe
  the Chief executive
Sainburys suppermarket
London town
Post code;;; Ec1N 2hT

Elsie Drake
Granville Gardens
Lodnon

29st August in 2018;;P

Dear Mr Coupe,

  i am 104 years old and the sixth oldest woman in Britin. I am Elsie Drake. I have been given a computor and it is narvellous. yesterday I learned how to do underlining and where the commas are,,,,,,,,,,,

Mr coupe, can you help me?

  I went to my Local "Sainsburys " suppermarket on Tuesday gone   to buy some cans of meat as I wanted to make a pie for my supper. I did not want Mrs Hale to have any cause she aways takes my pies when Im not looking and goes and   eats them in the toilet. She has a terrible appetite;; she once ate a whole hog for breakfast.

When I was in your shop i asked a lady where the meat cans were, but she said she was just shopping,so i asked a different lady but she was also a customer, so i asked a man in a nice shirt but he said that he didnt work there, but i didnt believe him cause he had the "airs" of a man who worked in a suppermarket, then i asked another lady but it was the same lady from before, so i asked a boy but he didnt understand cause he was only five , so I asked another man but it was the same man from earlier who didnt work there, so then i went home empty-handed.

  Mr Coupe, please can you tell me where the meat cans are so i can make a pie? i enclose five brittish pounds for your troubles. i am 104.

Remember;; where are all the meat cans?

Yours trully,

Elsie Drake

Elsie Drake (aged 104))

4 September 2018

Mrs Elsie Drake
Granville Gardens
London

Dear Mrs Drake,

Thank you for your letter dated 29th August which has been received into the Executive Office and read by Mike, he has requested that I look into your complaint and contact you personally.

I am sorry you were unable to locate a member of staff to assist you in finding the cans of meat you wanted to purchase.

I can advise as our local stores are smaller they do not hold our full range of products. In order for me to locate the items please could you confirm what type of meat you require and the size of tin. Once I have this I will reply directly to you by letter.

Please find enclosed the cash you provided.

Once again please accept my apologies and if I can be of any further assistance please contact me.

Kindest Regards

Nicola Haviland
Executive Office

Nicola Haviland
in the Execu tive ofice
Sainburys suppermarket
London
  EC1N 2H T

Elsie Drake
Granville Gardens
Lodnon

September 9st , 2018

  Dear Mrs or miss Haviland,

Thank you for your lovly letter it brought a smile to my face cause i do
not get many lelters these days. When I was younger, my late husband
Sidney used to write me letters a plenty. He once wrote me a letter from a
type of "box " he was trapped in.

  who put him there we will never know.

Lady, I have been trying to remember the type of meat can i was looking
for but just could not.   However , Mrs Hale made a meat casserole this
week and the meat tasted very similar to the one i normally buy in your
cans, so as you can see, i have put some of this meat in a little plastic tub
for you to taste.

  Maybe then you will know what can of meat is the one that tastes like
the meat that is in the little tub that originally came from Mrs Hales
casserole that tasted like the one I am looking for in cans .

The meat is fine to eat and is not spoiled.

Along with the meat i enclose five pounds monies for your help and i look
forward to knowing what the can of meat is that i wanted so i can go and
buy it from "Sainsburys Suppermarket "

Yours trully ,

Elsie Drake

Elsie Drake (aged 104)

25th September 2018

Mrs Elsie Drake
Granville Gardens
London

Dear Mrs Drake,

Thank you for replying to my letter.

I am sorry I am unable to taste the meat as it had deteriorated in the post. May I suggest you ask Mrs Hale for a list of the ingredients in the pie which may help us narrow down the possibilities.

Please find enclosed a cheque for the value of £7.00 to replace the money and the tub sent too as this has been disposed of.

Once again please accept my apologies and if I can be of any further assistance please contact me.

Yours sincerely

Nicola Haviland
Executive Office

the Manager,
The Red Rooms "gentlemens club",
  4 Great Queen Sreets,
Holborn,.
  London;' WC2 B 5Dg

Elsie Drake
Granville Gardens
Lodnon

August, 30yh 2018

Dear   sir or madams,

  I am 104 years old and and the 6th oldest woman in this country. My name is Elsie drake. Good day to you.

i have heard all about your magnificent dancing club from my great-grandson Nicolas who said that all the ladies there are very "confident dancers '. Well I am also a lady and I am also a confident dancer and I wonder if I could come and dance in your wonderful club. I can do these dances to a proficient standard:

Foxtrot
waltz
"Sway to the beat"
"Good time Lenny'
Normal dancing

  Mrs Hale told me not to write this letter she said that i will be made to look foolish when i dance and that the men will call me "beast"" and i will go home in tears. But she's the one whos   a beast, she is always eating biscuits and hiding them under her pillow,. One time she ate a whole packet of biscits while doing her busness on the toilet. i know because I saw the crumbs.

  i do not mind if men wolf- whistle at me. One time when I was with my late husband Sidney a man wolf-whistled and sidney climbed up the scafolding and punched the man so hard in his head, he had to go to hospital and have a blood transfixiation. it was a terrible time for me with a lot of mixed feelings.

  What music will you play for me and my dance? i will need something with a bit of "oomf to make an "impression" on the men, and   what sort of dancing do the ladies do in your dancing club?

I am sending you five english pound and I hope it covers my entrance costs.

Yours trully,

Elsie Drake

Elsie Drake (aged 104)

Mrs Elsie Drake
Granville Gardens
London

12 October 2018

Dear Mrs Drake

Thank you for your recent letter and interest in The Redrooms.

Your ballroom experience sounds a very good match for 'Strictly Come Dancing'.

Sadly we are not able to progress your letter further and so I am returning your £5 with our very best wishes for your future. As they say on Strictly . . . 'Keep Dancing!'

Best

Admin manager, Redrooms

Flora the margarine
   Upfield Uk ltimited
  FLORA
freepost ADM3940
London:: Sw1A 1Yr

Elsie Drake
Granville Gardens
Lodnon

is September the 1, 2018

Dear Flora margarine,

My name is Elsie Drake and I am 104 years of ag.e I am writing to you on a computor. It is plugged into walls.

  I have been eating your delicious margarine for 40 years. I think it has a lovly taste and I put it on everything such as bread, crumpets and wimples.

  can you help me Flora? Many years ago in 1935 I had my photograph taken by a man in Kent for a shilling. He told me to do a curtsy and a smile, and that my picture will be used on bottles of scouring powder;; I was very excited because i used to like scouring. but when I bought the scouring powder bottle my face was not there. it was just letters and information about scouring. I was very sad and i felt broken.

  in some ways i have never got over it.

Because i like flora so much and i am 104, would flora like to take my picture and put it on their margarine box? i have a lovely sweet smile and a nice eye, although Mrs Hale says my eye is too big but she is the one with the big eye.

Please let me me have my chance to shine and become a "flora girl". I am 104 and I want my face to be on the flora boxes.

I enclose £5 monies for your troubbles and a picture of the box with me on it . but can i has the picture back when you are done with it it is my ownly one .

Yours trully,

Elsie Drake

Elsie Drake (aged 104)

£ lora margarine

£10

Elsie Drake
is on the
box of the
margarine

The Flora box with Elsie
on it.

Can Elsie be on the
boxes?

Margarine

Elsie and Flor

Flora

Dear Elsie,

I wanted to write this little note to say thank you so much for the letter that you wrote us. It was great to take time out of my day to read it and it was fantastic to find out about your life experience with Flora!

Unfortunately, we are unable to accept the offer of using you for the cover of Flora as this is something that our Marketing Team look into after many months of research. All of the feedback that you have given us will be sent to them for future plans.

Thank you for making my day.

Yours sincerely,
Chris Browne

Mr. Chris Browne
   flora the Margarine, Upfield U.K
Freepost ADm3940
     London
     SW1A1Y R

Elsie Drake
Granville Gardens
Lodnon

On September the 10st, 2018

   Dear Mr. Browne from flora,

Thank you for your very kind letter with such beautiful handwriting. its elsie again and I wanted to be on the box of flora. Thankyou so much "Flora box with Elsie ".

I was so happy that the markets team said that they can make me go on the boxes. It is the happiest day of my life knowing that my face will adorn my beloved Flora boxes up and down the land, my fame will know no end .

Mrs Hale said that Flora would never allow my face on the boxes. She said my face was horrible and that it frightens pets, but my face has never frigtened pets. We used to have a pet dog called Shep and it was never frigtened by my face. it used to lick my nose in sheer joy. Shep was killed by cats.

   How do you get my face on the "Flora boxes";? Do they have to make a "print" of my face? Does it hurt ? Is it very hot ? How much does it cost? i enlcose five pounds as my deposit for the "Flora box with Elsie on it'

thank you again for the kindness you have shown me. I shall never forget it.

Yours truly .

Elsie Drake

Elsie Drake (aged 104))

Mrs Elsie Drake
Granville Gardens
London

Dear Mrs Drake,

Thank you for your recent comments to us here at Flora, and for providing your lovely story. We're delighted to hear that you love using Flora and really appreciate you taking the time to share your feedback. We always aim to produce products that are of the highest quality, so it's always fantastic to receive positive comments.

Unfortunately, we are unable to accept cash, so please find enclosed the £10 you sent to us.

Unfortunately, we do not have any current campaigns to put a face on tubs of Flora. However, if you would like to send us a photo, we would be happy to send you your own personalised tub.

Yours sincerely,

Christopher Browne
Unilever UK & Ireland Escalations Advisor

Mr Chris browne
Flora, the margarine .
Upfield U.K
 (freepost ADM 394o
London , post code;; sW1A1 YR

Elsie Drake
Granville Gardens
Lodnon

Septembor 19th 2018

Dear Mr Browne from Flora,

Thank you again for your letter. You are a very gracious man, I dont get much kind-ness at my age which is 104. Sir i was very happy that you will make me a special tub of "Flora with Elsie".

What is wrong with me being hapy? Nothing is wrong. why should it be wrong?

Mr Browne, I could not find any photographs of me cause of the terrible fire, but I have made a drawing instead of my like-ness.

I used be very good at drawing when I was younger. I even won an award from 'Lumptons Butchers" for my picture of a leg of lamb. It hung in their window for three weeks in 1934. Lumptons closed in 1937 cause Mr lumpton had been puting donkey meat in the mince. People said he should be hanged.

Thank you again for being so kind. I have enclosd a drawing of me that I did, and I look forward to seeing it on a "special tub for Elsie'.

Remember;; elsie is the "face of Flora" .

Yours trully,

Elsie Drake (aged 104)

"Special tub of Flora with Elsie"

To put
on the
"Flora Box"

← Elsie Drake
aged 104

Mrs Elsie Drake
Granville Gardens
London

Dear Mrs Drake,

Thank you for taking the time to contact us and to provide the drawing you were kind enough to send us. I have passed this drawing on to our internal marketing team. We will let you know once we receive their reply.

As previously advised, we are unable to accept cash from our consumers. With this in mind, please find enclosed the £5 note you sent us. Whilst we appreciate the gesture, please do not send us any more money.

We hope that you carry on enjoying Flora and thank you for your continued interest.

Yours sincerely,

Christopher
Unilever UK&I Escalations Advisor

Mr Chris Browne
The margarine "Flora "
upfield U.K.
   Freepost A.D.M 3940-
london SW1a 1YR

Elsie Drake
Granville Gardens
Lodnon

It is now 22 Nove,ber   2018

Dear Mr Browne,

I trust that you are very well and are enjoying working at Flora the margarine but I have still not recieved my "Special tub for Elsie" and it is nearly Christmas and i am 104 and it is cold and Mrs Hale banged her thorax and I am very worried my tub will not arrive in time for Yuletide .

Please will you ask the "Market" department to post my "tub"   with my picture to me as i would like to have it before I "go".

   I have written a little Christmas song for all of you who work so hard at the best magarine in the world which is called "Flora". Maybe you will sing it at your party but do not sing it too loud cause I have a smelly ear .

i also enclose a gift voucher for ten pounds monies from "Jon Lewis "" shops for your kindness and also for your Christmas . it was meant for Mrs Hale but I took it when she was sleeping.

Merry tidings to all good men and ladies

Yours trully,

Elsie Drake

Elsie Drake (aged 104)

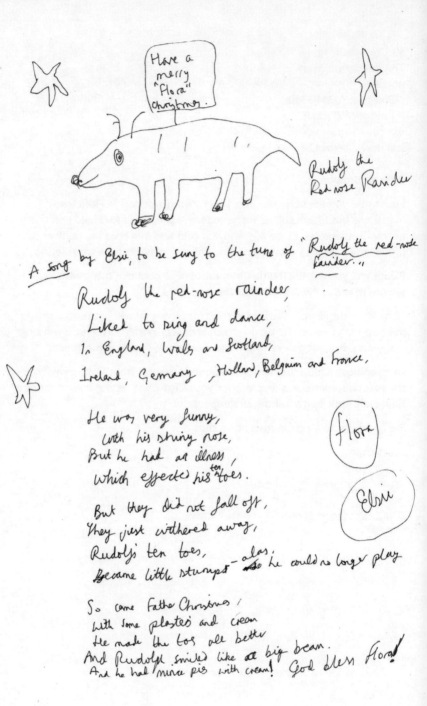

Have a merry "Flora" christmas.

Rudoly the Red nose Raindee

A song by Elsie, to be sung to the tune of "Rudoly the red-nose raindee."

Rudoly the red-nose raindee,
  Liked to sing and dance,
In England, Wales an Scotland,
Ireland, Germany, Holland, Belguim and France,

He was very funny,
  with his shiny nose,
But he had an illness,
which effected his ten toes.

But they did not fall off,
They just withered away,
Rudoly's ten toes,
Became little stumps - alas, he could no longer play

So came Father Christmas,
with some plasters and cream
He made the toes all better
And Rudolph smiled like a big beam.
And he had mince pies with cream! God bless Flora!

Flora

Elsie

TALK.GLOBAL

Mrs Elsie Drake
Granville Gardens
London

04th December 2018

Dear Mrs Drake,

We hope this letter finds you well and that you are having a good week to date. We are writing to you on behalf of Flora, please see below our reply to your most recent letter.

The below response has been curated,
With regards to your recent request,
For your face to be illustrated,
On one of our tubs, Flora is the best.

Whilst we would love to fulfil this ask for you Mrs Drake,
We are keen to *spread* your story far and wide,
and would really appreciate, if some time you could take,
to tell us your Flora story, we'll sure will delight and surprise.

If possible, could we give you a call,
On a phone number and time suitable to you,
To hear more about your quest to be printed,
On our tubs, and we'll see what we can do!

We look forward to receiving your reply, do please get in touch with the TALK.GLOBAL Flora team with any questions.

Kind regards, and all our best,

Sinead + The Full Flora Team
Sinead Lambe
Senior Account Executive

Sinead lambe
from Talk Global company
3,5 Rathbone place London
    london W12T1hHu

Elsie Drake
Granville Gardens
Lodnon

New year of 2019— January 18

Dear sinead Lambe,,

  thank you for your letter you posted to me back in the other year . it was an act of kindness that you wrote me a lovely poem and I am forever in your det even though I dont know who you are . Where is nice Mr Chris?

I am very sorry it has taken me so long to reply to you but i had an acident and burnt my legs because of where Mrs Hale left the toaster. Luckily I was seen by Dr Khartis   and his friend "Stefanie" and they applied creams but i had to rest for sevral weeks and keep my legs inverted .

minimal infection.

While i was inverted i found myself developing a taste for butter rather than margarine, so I now dont need my face stuck on a tub of "Flora". Instead i shall be writing to "Lurpack" to see if they will stick me on one of their butter tubs .

I still like Flora though and i will never forget it.

Yours trully,

Elsie Drake

Elsie Drake (aged 104)

NO MORE LETTERS

Matthew Gould,
in charge of
London Zoo,
Outer Circle
London nw1, 4RY

Elsie Drake
Granville Gardens
Lodnon

month March 13th, yera 2023.

Dear Mr. Gould ,

My name is Elsie Drake and i am 104 years old and the sixth oldest woman in the united Kingdomf. I am writing on a computor so please wish me luck,

good luck elsie

Dear sir, I think one of your aninals may have escaped from your zoo. Last week i fround a hedge-hog in my garden and I do not know how is got there or where it came from. My friend Bessie Bates told me hedgehogs are only kept in London zoo because its the law. Is it your hedge-hog? If it is yours do I have to bring it back? but how will i do that? I am 104 .

Mrs Hale said that hedgehogs are "native to Britin" but Bessie said that they are "only native to the zoos of this land' "No they are not Bessie' Mrs hale said, "they are" "they are not you fool" They are" "shut up you filth" "dont call me that" . It was a terrible agument and when i woke up, Bessie was crying and Mrs Hale was no-where to be seen. Did you see her?

Mr Gould, Is it true that all "hedge-hogs" in this land belong to your zoo? I hope not cause I have grown quite attached to the little beast. Am I allowed to call it 'Potsy'?   or is it the law that I have to call it just "hedgehog" .i want to call it Potsy.

Please write back. i am 104 and want to know if i can keep Potsy of if i have to give it to you cause   of British law. i have enclosed five pounds to help you all .

i have drawn a picture of Potsy but please can you send it back so I can put it on walls .

Yours trully,

Elsie Brake

Elsie Drake (aged 104)

Elsie Drake found a "hedge-hog"

"Potsy"
the hedge-hog"

mud blocks
— they are in
the garden.
Mr Lynford said he
will remove them on the 6th

I gave it
a banana
but it
shunned it.

ZSL
Zoological
Society
of London

15 May 2023

Mrs Elsie Drake
Granville Gardens
London

Dear Elsie,

Thank you for your wonderful letter. I am so pleased you found a hedgehog and can confirm that there is no legal impediment to you calling it 'Potsy'. In fact, I think this is an excellent name for your hedgehog, and if anyone – including Mrs Hale and Bessie Bates – should criticise your choice of name, please inform them that the Chief Executive of The Zoological Society of London has given it his strong endorsement.

I can also confirm that London Zoo does not own all the hedgehogs in the country, although we are very interested in making sure their numbers flourish, and that the species does not go extinct. I may be mistaken, but my understanding is that in strict legal terms, they are all owned by the Archbishop of Canterbury, even though the Roman Catholic Archbishop of Westminster also lays claim to them and has done ever since the schism from Rome in 1534.

That said, hedgehogs are wild animals, and so my advice would be to let Potsy roam free. If you leave out suitable food for Potsy, he (or she) may well become a regular visitor.

I am sorry that Potsy shunned your banana. In fact, hedgehogs mostly eat insects and other invertebrates. In the wild, they would eat beetles, earwigs, caterpillars, earthworms, and so on. You could feed Potsy meat-based cat or dog food, and you should also leave out a shallow dish of water as well.

I hope this answers your hedgehog-based questions. Thank you so much for the £5 donation, which we will use for conserving hedgehogs and other threatened animal species. As you requested, I am also sending you back the wonderful picture of Potsy.

Yours Sincerely,

Matthew Gould,
Chief Executive Officer, ZSL

"The Peoples Friend" magazine for older Readers;
   Letters page
   2 Albert Square, Dundee
post code: DD1 1DD

Elsie Drake
Granville Gardens
Lodnon

March 19, 2023

Dear "The peoples friend" magazine .

   My name is Elsie Drake and i am 104 years of age and i have been learning to type on a computor. i think it is wonderful,, dont you? Why cant an older lady use a computor? There is nothing wrong with that. I should be allowed, and i am.

Sir or madam, I have been reading your lovely magazine "the Peoples Friend" for over fifty years now, and i cherish every issue. It brightens up my day no end. Thank you for your kindness both of you. Without it i would be bereft,.

I am writing to tel you that at 104 i have just started going to art classes. My teacher is "Lynne" . I find it a wonderful experiense. When i put pen to paper my mind drifts back to when I were a little girl playing in the road with Clemence and Lily. They were the happiest days of my life. Once a rogue pig wandered into our road from the fields and ate Lilys clogs!

It has always been my dream to have a letter publihsed in your "Peoples' Friend " magazine, and i am enclosing my first ever self-portrate of myself for you to print if you like it. Will you put it in the magazine? It would make me so proud. i will die a happy lady.

   Please let me have my chance to shine   and i thank you again for your glorious magazine "the Peoples friend"

Yours trully ,

Elsie Drake (aged 104)

Between Friends

Write to us at Between Friends, "The People's Friend", 2 Albert Square, Dundee DD1 1DD, or e-mail us at betweenfriends@dcthomson.co.uk.

Star Letter

My name is Elsie Drake. I'm one hundred and four years of age and I've been learning to type on a computer.

I think it is wonderful – why can't an older lady use a computer?

I've been reading your magazine for over fifty years now and I cherish every issue. It brightens up my day no end, I can tell you.

I'm writing to tell you that at my age I have just started going to art classes. I find it a wonderful experience.

When I put pen to paper, my mind drifts back to when I was a little girl. They were the happiest days of my life.

It has always been my dream to have a letter published in "The People's Friend" and I am enclosing my first-ever self portrait of myself for you to print. I hope you put it in the magazine.

I would be so proud and very happy. Thank you again for your glorious magazine.

Mrs E.D., London.

Our Star Letter writer will receive a Dean's branded shopping bag containing a selection of delicious Dean's shortbread.
Consume as part of a balanced diet. Prize may vary slightly from picture.

All other printed UK letters will win one of our famous tea caddies and a pack of loose tea. Our friends from overseas will receive an alternative prize.

NO MORE LETTERS

Mrs Penny Mordaunt ;
the head of the Privy Council
Room G/04,
1 horse Guards Road
London. Sw1 a 2HQ

Elsie Drake
Granville Gardens
Lodnon

March, 21, st 2023

Dear Mrs Mordaunt,

My name is Elsie Drake and i am 104 years of age and also the sixth oldest woman in Britin. It is nice to "meet you" . I am using a computor unit right now. Do you use a computor unit?

buzzing sound from the machine

Madam, I do not know what the Privy council is exacly but I believe you have something to do with the goverment and also with information that you are "privy" to. If that is correct, here is some infomation you might find very interesting. Its all about Mrs Hale.

1). Sometimes Mrs hale whistles "lewdly" when she is in the bath. Once Mr Lunnock bung on the wall with his brick to make her stop, but to no avail. Mr Lunnock now lives in Wessex he has moved.

2. Mrs Hale thinks she can swim like a profesional, but all she does is make a mess with the water going in peoples eyes and ears, and once it went in a nose.

4) Mrs Hale confuscated my earwig last week. Id kept it in a matchbox for over forty years but it is no longer alive. This morning i found out where she is keeping it. Would you like to know the exact location? I could draw a map for you maybe.

Madame, I have lots more interesting information about Mrs Hale such as medical details dating back over thirty years. Would you like me to send you this sort of information on a regular basis?. I could be the Privy Council's "spy". I could write to you in invisbal ink. Do the privy council use invisibal ink?

Please let me have my chance to shine. I would like to be useful to society and I am 104. I enclose five pounds for any troubles caused.

Yours truly,

Elsie Drake (aged 104)

Mrs Elsie Drake
Granville Gardens
London

18th April 2023

Dear Mrs Drake,

Thank you for your letter addressed to the Rt Hon Penny Mordaunt MP, Lord President of the Privy Council, which has been passed to me for reply.

I have to inform you that this is not a matter in which the Lord President is able to be involved. I also return your £5.

Yours sincerely,

Privy Council Office

Mr Archie Norman, the Chair-man
  Marks and Specer shops
waterside House
35, north Wharr road,, Londdon
W2,1NW (post code)

Elsie Drake
Granville Gardens
Lodnon

The day is 3 April, year 2023

Dear mr Norman,

   I am 104 years old and the sixth oldest woman in this land. My name is
Elsie Drake. This letter is being written on a computor . Why can't i write
on a computor at my age? what is wrong with that? If the goverment
allows it i can do it.

   Sir, i worked in Marks and spencer shops   in Marble arch in London back
in 1945. i was in the department that sold "beaks" for a gentleman named
Mr Whittock. He had one ear but he was as kind as an ox. it was a
wondeful time. everyone was so kind to me. thank you.

Can you help me please ? I lost my pewter ring in your shop on my last
day of work which was August 24, 1946. it was given to me by my blessed
mother Daisy Toddley and ingraved with my name which is Elsie and i
have never forgotten it. i cried for days when it was gone, "stop crying
Elsie " they said but I could not stop.

Would you be able to see if you still have it somwhere in your shops?
Maybe it's in a box or a bag or a basket or a cabinet ? Does Mark and
Spencer still have cabinets? Mr Whittock used to keep his packd lunch in a
cabinet;; sardine sandwiches, an aple,   and some milk prisms .

Can you fine my ring please? I am 104 and it is my one desire to find that
poor innocent ring before i "go".

i enclose five pounds for your help in finding my presious beautiful ring.

Yours trully,

Elsie Drake

Elsie Drake (ages 104 ,)

M&S

EST. 1884

Mrs Elsie Drake
Granville Gardens
London

3rd May 2023

Dear Elsie,

Thank you for your letter to our Chairman, Archie Norman. My name is Martyn and I am the store manager at Marble Arch. Archie has asked me to respond to you personally.

It was great to read about some of your fond memories of working at M&S with Mr Whittock and your other colleagues. I can fully appreciate how disappointing it must have been to lose your precious ring on your last day with M&S. Myself and my team have taken time to look across the store, in many different places.

As you can imagine, our shop has undergone many changes in the past 76 years and I am sorry to say we have been unable to find your ring.

I'm so sorry that whilst this is the news you may have expected, it is not the answer either of us would have hoped for.

I have been in contact with our company archive which is based in Leeds and have been able to find some pictures of Marble Arch from 1945/46 which I have enclosed with this letter.

Whilst no substitute for your ring, I hope some of them bring back some happy memories of your time working with us.

I have also enclosed your £5 note that you included with your letter.

If I can help with anything further, please do feel free to contact me personally.

Yours Sincerely

Martyn Carr
Store Manager

Mr Martin   Carr, store Manager
at Marble arch,
   Marks and Specer shop
458, Oxford street,
L ondon W1C, 1 ap

Elsie Drake
Granville Gardens
Lodnon

8 ,June 2023

Dear Mr Carr,

   Thank you for writinf back to me all about my lost pewter ring. You are
an honour-able gentleman sir with much kindness .

   The lovly pictures you sent brouhgt back wonderful memories, but i
could not believe it when i saw the picture with the ladies in it, cause the
lady in the bottom corner on the right who is looking at a bit of paper,
that is me !,

When i showed it to Mrs Hale she said it cant be me because the lady was
"pretty not like you". I told her that i was a real beauty in those days and
that I was the "bell of the ball ". but Mrs Hale did not like that cause she
was never the bell of the ball.

   never.

I think the paper i am looking at in the picture is the stock list, and Im
checking it to see which beak is in or out of stock. Mr Whittock would
check all my checking, and on Fridays he gave me a bun from Craddocks
the   bakers . i loved those buns .

   Perhaps you could hold an exhibition in the Marks and Spencer shop all
about my life . It will be a wonderful day, I will remember it for the rest of
my life. But I will need to know when it is so i am not late for my
exhibition. Also,   will you invite dignatries?

Will there be an exhibition about Elsie ? I enclose £ 5, for your   help and
thank you again .

Yours trully,

Elsie Drake

Elsie Drake (aged, 104)

Mrs Elsie Drake
Granville Gardens
London

23rd June 2023

Dear Elsie,

Thank you for your letter. I am so pleased you enjoyed seeing the pictures and I'm sorry again that we were unable to find your ring.

I can only imagine how surprised you were when you recognised yourself in one of the pictures. A truly special moment, considering the number of people who would have worked with us at that time.

I'm sure you have many happy stories to share of your time at M&S, however I'm afraid we won't be able to hold an exhibition.

Thank you again for getting in touch and I'm really pleased to have been able to re-unite you with some great memories of your time at M&S, ones which I hope you continue to cherish.

I have enclosed the £5 note that you sent with your letter.

Yours Sincerely

Martyn Carr
Store Manager

Mr Martin carr,
Store Manager of Marble Arch,
  Marks and Specer shop
458, Oxford St. Street
London, W1C, 1AP.

Elsie Drake
Granville Gardens
Lodnon

July.24. 20.23

Dear Mr Martin,

Thank you for your wonderful letter but I am very sory cause I thought the lady in the picture was me but i made a terible mistale cause it wasn't me. there was a lady called Freda who worked the tills who people remarked looked similar to me, and it was her .

  Freda had a sharp tongue on her, mind , she once shouted at me in front of mr Whittock and called me a "Basin Babe" which was terible slander in those days. The basin she refered to were ones used by farmers to wash their filthy hands in. I believe there was even a song by Miriam Lenby called "I'll never be your Basin Babe" . it was a very sad song cause the lady in it   accidently drinks the wretched water in the basin and gets . Lymes disease. The song was very popular in my day although i was never that fond of it . i didnt like the trumpits, they were too shrill.

  do you like trumpits?

I am looking forward to the exhibition on October 1st all about my life in your shop, but If you dont mind, when we are at the exhibition, Id actualy like to tell people that the lady in the picture is in fact me and not Freda. That way i will be the bell of the ball.   So remember, please do not tell people that it is not me and tell them it is me . i will forever be grateful .

  I cannot wait for the "Elsie exhibition" and will be counting down the days. i have enclosed a poster you can put up in your shops.

  Thank you for all your kindness.

yours trully,

Elsie Drake

  Elsie Drake (aged 104.)

ELSIES Escibition at "Marks and Spencer"

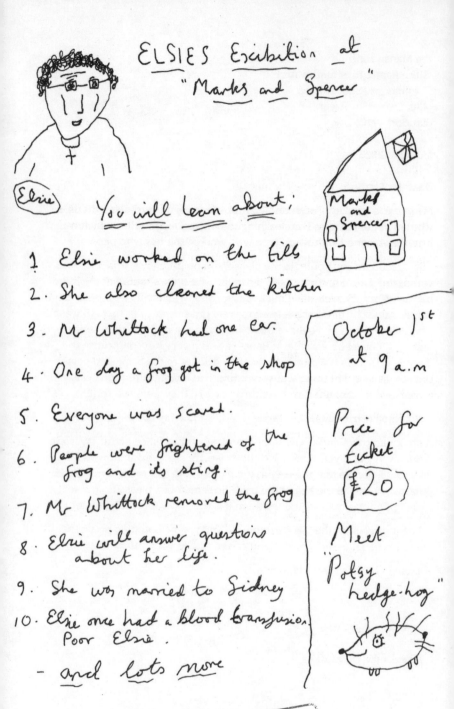

Elsie

You will learn about;

1. Elsie worked on the tills

2. She also cleaned the kitchen

3. Mr Whittock had one ear.

4. One day a frog got in the shop

5. Everyone was scared.

6. People were frightened of the frog and its sting.

7. Mr Whittock removed the frog

8. Elsie will answer questions about her life.

9. She was married to Sidney

10. Elsie once had a blood transfusion. Poor Elsie.

 - and lots more

October 1st at 9 a.m

Price for Ticket £20

Meet "Potsy hedge-hog"

NO MORE LETTERS

the Manager of
   The Range furniture shops
   William prance Raod,,
plymouth ;
pL6, 5ZD

Elsie Drake
Granville Gardens
Lodnon

1, 1 June 2023

Dear the Range furniture shop manager ;

My name is Mrs Elsie Drake and I am 104 years of age and the sixth oldest woman in the country. I am learning to write on a computor which has just been cleaned with a rag .

   Sir or madam can you help me please?   I bought a lovly sofa from your wonderful shop a few years ago but i think the sofa is haunted.   This is because a spirit called the "Pink Lady" seems to live inside it , and only comes out at night to   scare me witless .

the "Pink lady" is dressed all in pink , even her face is pink and her bonnet too.   She also wears pink tites.   The pink Lady is a terible ghoul.

Did i buy a haunted sofa by mistake? The man didnt say it was haunted by a ghost when i bought it.

   What do i do now? Maybe the Pink Lady should be "excorsized " as   she is a menace. She sometimes shouts rude words at me while i sleep , "pig," "dirty   bottom; " "Hussy of the night " and such the like. it is not nice.

Do you do excorcisms at the Range shops? And do you use goat blood in your ceremony? or should i just burn the sofa?

Remember – can you get rid of the "Pink lady "? i enclose five pound £5.

You are my only hope. i am 104.

Yours trully,

Elsie Drake

Elsie Drake (aged 104)

The Terifying "Pink Lady"

Bonnet (pink)

glasses (pink)

hair (pink)

face (all of it is pink)

Jumper (pink)

Buttons (these are blue)

skirt (it is pink)

tites (also pink)

shoes (even they are pink)

Mrs Elsie Drake
Granville Gardens
London

Dear Mrs. Drake,

Firstly, I would like to thank you for taking the time for sending a letter regarding your sofa.

Whilst I do understand that you feel that you would like some assistance with your sofa, ourselves here at The Range would be unable to help should you feel your sofa may be haunted.

In reference to your question regarding whether you should burn your sofa, I can confirm that we would advise strongly against this and confirm we do not use goats blood in the production of our sofas.

As I can see that you have kindly sent us £5.00 should we be able to help with the issue you had raised, please see this re-enclosed in your letter.

I apologise that we were unable to provide the services you have requested and hope that you are able to come to an amicable resolution with the Pink Lady.

Kindest regards,

The Range Customer Care Team Head Office

to The Chariman,
   of   Greggs bakery
quorum busness Park ,
   Newcatestle upon Tyne Post code;; NE128bu

Elsie Drake
Granville Gardens
Lodnon

3d June 2023

Dear Chairman.

   My name is Elsie Drake and I am   104 years of age and the sixth oldest woman in this country.

   i am very fond of your food in Greggs, it is so tasty.   Yesterday i had one of your sausage pies and then gave a tiny piece to my hedge-hog "Potsy" . Thank you gregg.

I am writinf to tell you that my grandmother Eleanor Toddley god rest her soul, used to make beautiful little pies called '"Priests fingers" each Whitsun . Priests Fingers   are shaped like fingers cause that is their name, and in them is canned tuna,   minced beef,, bits of bread and a little piece of banana. They are delicious.

I think Priests fingers would be lovly in Greggs shops for people to buy and eat them,   so I have made one for you and your staff to eat, and have enclosed it in this letter in a plastic tin. My husband Sidney used to eat a couple of fingers in his bed every night when he was living. He loved those fingers . poor Sidney.

If you like the taste will you put my priests fingers in your Greggs shops up and down the land?   Maybe you could also let me could cook them "on site". I will be a very happy lady and my fame will be limit-less.

I am enclosing five pounds along with the lovely priests finger for any inconvenienses but can you send me back my tin please, as its the one i normally keep my food in for Potsy . Thank you Gregg.

Yours truly,

Elsie Drake

Elsie Drake (aged 104)

Elsie's "Priest's finger"
(tuna, beef and banana)

Mrs Elsie Drake
Granville Gardens
London

07 June 2023

Dear Elsie

Thank you for getting in touch with our Chairman. We have a dedicated team of people in Customer Care who are here to respond to your requests. This is so that we can help to continuously improve the service we offer.

We really love to hear from our customers. It is great to hear that you are so passionate about us and what we do.

Your idea of a bake made with Tuna, Beef, Bread pieces and Banana is a good one!

Although we cannot promise that we will be able to introduce this, we have passed your valuable feedback on to our Retail Team for their consideration. They will take this on board at their next review.

As a gesture of goodwill, please find below a code for £5.00 to be used in our shops (excluding some Franchise shops & Iceland).

Please also find enclosed Potsy's food box along with your £5.00 and pre-paid envelope.

Once again, thank you for getting in touch with our Chairman. We hope to see you in our shops again soon, Elsie.

Yours Sincerely

Kerry
Customer Care Team

to Kerry
    Customer care team;; Greggs
of Gregg Bakery
Quorum Business park,
    Newcastle _Upon _Tyne
NE128BU;

Elsie Drake
Granville Gardens
Lodnon

15,; June 2023

Dear Kerry.

Thank you very very much for writing back to me wth your lovly letter and i was so happy that you liked my "Priests finger" pie and that Greggs are going to put Priests fingers in the shops.   Will i get a penny a pie?

Kind Kerry, I am enclosing a different pie I have made that I think Gregg will also want to sell. It is called "lunny pie" and it is another of my blessed grandmothers recipes. Lunnies contain beautiful suet and kidney, some cheese and a little piece of banana. They are delisious.

i gave one to Mrs Hale but she said it tasted of dung   so do not listen to her. When she was busy doing her legs, I put a worm in her bed. The worm is alive.

 i hope you enjoy the taste of my lunny and i look forward to hearing from you. Maybe when Gregg sells them i can get two pennies a lunny? Thank you for your kindness and i tihink Greggs is a nice shop. i enclose five pounds for costs.

Yours trully,

Elsie Drake

Elsie Drake (aged, 104)
   P-S please can you return my little bowl in which Ive put my lunny as i need it to make more lunnies.

Elsie's "lunny"
(suet, kidney, cheese
and banana)

Mrs Elsie Drake
Granville Gardens
London

22 June 2023

Dear Elsie

Thank you for taking the time to get back to us with another of your homemade bakes.

We've again passed your suggestion on to our Retail Team, however we're unable to guarantee that we'll introduce these into our shops.

Please find enclosed your £5.00 and your pie dish. Unfortunately, we'll not be able to return any further items to you by post in future.

Once again, thanks for getting in touch with us, Elsie. We hope to see you in our shops again soon.

Yours Sincerely

Kerry
Customer Care Team

The head of Drama televission
the BBC,,
Bbc Drama village
1020, Bristol road
Birmingham, B29, 6IG

Elsie Drake
Granville Gardens
Lodnon

June 6; 2023

Dear BBC,

My name is Elsie Drake and i am 104 years old and the sixth oldest woman in Britin. I have been using a computor to write this. I am very sorry if i make mistakes but i am determined to get used to computor machines . They are important in all our lives elsie.

It has always been my dream to have my own programe on the television,   and so i have written a script for a new programme called 'Elsies Day" and it is all about my days i have. Well, wouldnt people want to see what a 104 year old lady does to fill her days? i certainly would and i am already 104 !

sinus treatment with dr Navros

I have   enclosed a cupple of pages of the script for "Elsies Day" . I have never writen a television   script before so please be kind.   Did you like it?

If you did then when do we make it? Do we film it at the BBC ? Will I have to wear costumes? What sort of costumes will they be? I hope they are nice costumes, i am sorry for all the questions but I am just very excited to be making "Elsies Day'.

Please let me have my chance to shine. Thank you . I enclose five pounds .

Yours trully,

Elsie Drake (aged 104)

ELSIES DAY – page 1/ of the script by Elsie drake age, 104

Elsie is inside her house.
Elsie: Hello my name is Elsie and iam 104 and the sixth oldest woman in Britin. I hope you enjoy the programme

Elsie then finishes getting drssed. She walks to the kitchen and made some tea.

Elsie; I always start my mornings with a nice cup of tea.

She has a sip but then there are knocks at the door.

Elsie : Who is it?
She opened the door and it is just the postman, his name is Bill . Elsie and Bill have known each other for 6 months and so are very close

Bill : hello elsie
Elsie: hello Bill. Did you get my letters?
Bill; yes, they are in my bag. Here

HE PASSED THE LETERS TO HER
Elsie reads the letters out loud. But we only hear one of them read, it is the most importent one

Elsie : Dear Mrs Drake, you have been requested by law to go to the police station because you are wanted for murder .
Elsie is very shocked.

Elsie;;Murder? I never murdered anyone in my life

Bill: I cant believe they wrote that. That is so strange. Well, goodbye Elsie

Elsie;Goodbye.

Elsie WALKS INTO THE KITCHEN AFTER SHE SHUT THE FRONT DOOR>

Elsie: i must finish my tea. I never murdered anyone. It must be a case of mis-taken identity.

Then it is at the POLiCE station.

Policeman – We are so sorry Elsie but we made a mistake with the letter. It was not you who did the murder it was Mr Paul Linn who is a local dentist. He has been a dentist for nearly thrity years but he got angry and killed one of his patients for having terible teeth

Elsie That is awful ,and what did the murderer do for a living?

Policeman: he was a profesional dentist

LATER ON ELSIE MEETS A KIND LOCAL RESIDENT WHO OFFERS TO CARRY HER SHOPPING BUT DUE TO PRIDE SHE SAYS "NO I DONT NEED YOUR HELP"

OTHER THINGS THAT CAN HAPPEN IN THE PROGRAME;
loses her keys
bangs head but does not go to hospitel
    umbrella breaks
Makes phone calls
Makes pie for dinner, It is deliicious !
Discovers another murderer and calls the police

BUT DID THEY AREST THE RIGHT MAN THIS TIME ,? Find out in "Elsies Day".

Hi Elsie!

Thanks so much for your letter, and for your script! We really enjoyed it, although we were worried that Elsie was going to be arrested for murder!

We were also very impressed by your computer skills.

Unfortunately we cannot accept unsolicited scripts, and we cannot accept your donation – but thank you, we are very grateful.

I have enclosed your script and the five pounds here for you.

Thank you again for taking the time to write to us.

All the best,

Production Secretary

The manager of
    Warwick Castle,
Warwick, warwick,
Cv34, 4QU

Elsie Drake
Granville Gardens
Lodnon

June 23::; 2023

Dear Sir or madam,

   My name is Elsie Drake and i am 104 and the sixth oldest woman in Britin. I was delighted to win the competition for a weekend stay with friends at "warwick Castle" and so here are the names of all my friends who will be staying with me.

My friends:
Doris Michaels (aged 99 ,)
Hilda Finnigan, (aged 96)
Alice Dunn   (i dont know her age)
   Bessie Bates (aged 99,)
   Violet Crub, (she says she is 90 but Doris thinks she is at least 95 cause of her neck.   )
Hilda Rogers (aged 97)
Joyce Bunty (aged 95)
The Langley twins, (Nora and Nancy who are both aged 94 and never married)
Mr Ralf Groberts (age 100) he is a nice met i have met   but he wont eat any turkey
Mrs Hale – she is definitly not coming

   The activities we would like to do over the weekend are:
Armour-wearing
Musket ball firing
"Bait the horses"
Feasting with "Michael" Who is Michael by the way?
Combat skills

   I am still unclear as to how you are going to transport us to your castle as I have heard nothing back from you. Where do you colect us from? Will we be traveling by coach or box-ferry? Please could you let me know as soon as posible as the weekend is fast approaching. We are all very excited.I   enclose £5.

Yours trully,

Elsie Drake (aged 104)

WARWICK
✤ CASTLE ✤

Dear Elsie

Thank you for your lovely letter, I am so pleased to hear that you and your friends are fit and getting out and about.

Unfortunately I fear that you may have been misled about winning a competition at Warwick Castle; I have confirmed with colleagues that we have not run any such competition to stay with friends. Not knowing how this was communicated to you I am unable to investigate it any further. I hope this is not too much of a disappointment to you.

I am returning your £5 and also a replacement stamp.

With very best wishes to you and your friends.

Guest Services

NO MORE LETTERS

The manager,
Puzzler Magazine,
" Puzzler media" Ltd
3r d floor of Fonteyn House
   47-49 London Road,
reigate, RH2, 9PY

Elsie Drake
Granville Gardens
Lodnon

24June2023

Dear   Puzzler magazine,

   You are my favrite magazine in the world and I am called Elsie Drake
and I am 104 years of age and i am the sixth oldest woman in Britin.
"Puzzler magazine" is lovly, I read it all the time and do all the puzzles

Word-searching

searching for the words

The only problem is Mrs Hale keeps taking my "Puzzler magazine" and
filling in all the words her-self, so when she is asleepi fill in her knitting
magazine "The Knitting Lady". I draw all over the pages.

Dear Puzler,   i am writing to you on a computor because it would be a
dream come true if I could have my own page of puzles in Puzzler. It is
called "Elsies Corner ".   I love making puzzles and search-words and i
think your readers will enjoy Elsies corner, which is a page by Elsie Drake
who is 104. After all, when have they ever seen that before? They havent.

I have enclosed a page i made with some exampals of my wondeful
puzzles, but please excuse any mess as i am 104 and sometimes cannot
get enough purchase on the pen. Do you like my puzzles? Will you let me
have a page for "Elsies corner" ? Please give me my chance to shine . You
are a very kind magazine,

i am sending you £5 to cover office costs. Is this too little? But why do you
need my money? Thank you "Puzzler Magazine" for all the puzzles.

   Yours truly,

Elsie Drake (aged 104)

Elsie's Puzzle Corner
by Elsie Drake, 104

WORD-SEARCH

```
E L S I E
L E E D S
S A D L Y
I B B I N
E L Y B Y
```

Can you find these words?

ELSIE
SEDBY
IDLIB
LEEDS
SADLY
ELYBY
ESYNY
~~CARDI~~
IBBIN

POTSY'S PUZZLE

CAN YOU help "Potsy Hedge-hog" find his way to his metal cage?

But which number route does he take??

1
2.
3

Potsys metal cage

ELSIES "BRAIN-TICKLER"

am twice the size of a hotel that is famous for its food and also I have wheels but must never be moved. If you call me, I will not come. I also eat onions. WHAT AM I?

Answer next week

PRIZE
£10,000

Puzzler®

Mrs Elsie Drake
Granville Gardens
London

20 July 2023

Contribution to Puzzler magazine

Dear Elsie,

Huge thanks to you for sending us your wonderful puzzles; we were impressed by your creations, especially the lovely drawing of Potsy. So much so, that we've decided to include this in our editor's introduction on page 3 of Puzzler, issue 647, on sale 13 September. We'll send you a copy when it's out – we are making an edition especially for you that contains your puzzles!

We wanted to let you know that your letter brought everyone in the company so much joy and so we are enclosing some free magazines for you – perhaps you'd like to pass on one of the wordsearch magazines to Mrs Hale in the hope it might stop her filling in your magazines? We have to say we very much enjoyed reading about the mischief you both seem to get up to with each other's magazines!

We are returning your puzzles as requested, plus the £5 and stamped, self-addressed envelope. Perhaps you could put them to use elsewhere.

Thank you once more, Elsie, for lighting up our lives with your special puzzles and tales of your intrepid antics when Mrs Hale is asleep.

Your riddle has foxed us all so we think your £10,000 prize is safe! Perhaps you could drop us another line, or give us a call to reveal the answer, we'd love a chat with you.

Your creativity and sense of fun at 104 years old is an inspiration to everyone here at Puzzler!

With all best wishes,

Shameem Begg
Promotions & Innovations Manager
Puzzler Media
Encs.

Shameem Begg,
puzzler magazine
" Puzzler   Media" ltd,
3rd Floor,, Fonteyn House;[
47-49 london Road,
Reigate. RH,2, 9PY

28 July 202,3

Dear Shameem Begg,

Thank you for your glorious letter. if you remember, i was the lady that
sent you "Elsies Corner " which was a piece of paper full of wonder-ful
puzzles. Well I was delighted to read that you are putting my puzles in
your beautiful magazine. Thank you "Puzzler " for all the kindness you
have shown me.

   I am looking forward to the "date of publication" and   I will be holding a
littel party to celebrate. Everyone will be there, Bessie bates of course ,
also my friend Violet Crub if she is better, cause she bit into a sandwich
last week that had a nail in it. It was terrible.   Mrs Hale will be there
unfortinatly but luckily "Potsy" my lovly hedge-hog will be in attendance .

Will you be at the party?

   Yours trully,

Elsie Drake

Elsie Drake (aged 104).

Ps You asked me to tell you the answer to my riddle but Im sory but Ive
forgotten it. Maybe the answer was "British Steel" ?

Welcome to *Puzzler* 647!

Here at Puzzler, we sometimes receive letters almost too good to be true... We received a lovely letter this week from an avid *Puzzler* reader, Elsie, who's 104 years old and a puzzle-solving pro. Elsie even sent in some of her own wonderful puzzles, including a wordsearch, a riddle and a tangled lines puzzle, proving it's never too late for us to get in touch with our creative sides! We especially love Elsie's character Potsy the Hedgehog, which I've included below.

I wanted to shine a light on the joy Elsie brought everyone at Puzzler when we received her letter. It included a brilliant anecdote about Mrs H, another puzzle enthusiast, who likes to borrow Elsie's copy of *Puzzler* and fill in the words herself – so when Mrs H is asleep, Elsie fills in another of Mrs H's magazines in return! Who knew Puzzler would be the centre of such a marvellous scandal?

Elsie, if you're reading, we are thrilled and delighted that you continue to enjoy *Puzzler* and that you are a shining example of a lifelong puzzle enthusiast. I'll do my best to keep making the best puzzles possible for you and all our readers, whom we appreciate so much. Knowing the joy it brings you makes the work we do feel even more worthwhile.

Please make sure to check out the Big Cash Competition on page 17. The prizes total **£6,000** and it's free to enter, so enjoy!

Make it a great month,

Tim

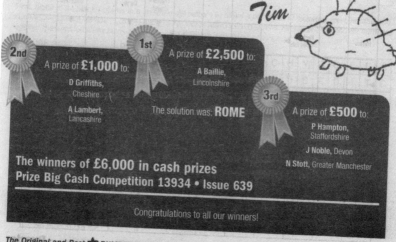

2nd

A prize of **£1,000** to:

D Griffiths,
Cheshire

A Lambert,
Lancashire

1st

A prize of **£2,500** to:

A Baillie,
Lincolnshire

The solution was: **ROME**

3rd

A prize of **£500** to:

P Hampton,
Staffordshire

J Noble, Devon

N Stott, Greater Manchester

The winners of £6,000 in cash prizes
Prize Big Cash Competition 13934 • Issue 639

Congratulations to all our winners!

The Original and Best ★ BUMPER ISSUE

NO MORE LETTERS

The person in charge of
  Walls
Corinium avenue
Gloucester
  postal codal; GI4 3DU

Elsie Drake
Granville Gardens
Lodnon

June 25 ,. 2023

Dear person in charge of walls,

Good morning it is Elsie Drake here and I am 104 years of age and the sixth oldest woman in this country. Congratulations, I never thought i would reach this age when i was a baby. In those days I went around in a cloth nappie and my mother, god bless her soul would wash it in the gully outside. My father was no good he never helped with my swaddling   or with my ablutions

Sir or madam, Mrs hale told me that you are the correct person to write to all about walls , as I have a dredful poblem with them.   Parts of my walls feel very dry, and other parts feel very wet. How do i get my walls to feel all normal again? in other words, I want walls that are not too dry and not too wet ?

  Mrs hale told me my walls need to be rubbed down hard with vinegar, so she's got me on my hands and knees at all hours scrubbing them with the "Sarsons" that i normally use on my chips.

Can you help Elsie?   What is the answer to this terible predicament?   is it vinegar?

Thank you for all your kind help in this intricate matter, and i send you £5 for your assistance with the walls.

Your trully,

Elsie Drake

Elsie Drake (aged 104.)

Hi Elsie

You need a different company as Walls is an Ice Cream company

Your

Person in charge

The manager of
  Wimpy Burgers Restraunts
2, The Listons, ,
Liston road in Marlow
SL7,1FD

Elsie Drake
Granville Gardens
Lodnon

26, June 2023

Dear Wimpy Burgers manager,

My name is Elsie Drake and I am 104 years of age and the sixth oldest woman in Britin. Please excuse my errors but I am doiing this on a computor. I am "computoring" right now,.

Wimpy manager, I wanted to let you know that I ate a wimpy burger in "Wimpy burgers" last week with my friend Bessie Bates and also Mrs hale who is not really my friend. Anyway my wimpy burger was really lovly. the bun was soft, the meat was also soft but also nice, Bessie had two burgers and she also said that the bun and the meat in it were soft. Mrs hale just had some water.

Onto the chips now, they were lovly and soft too. Bessie had three portions and all of them were also soft according to her. Mrs hale didnt have chips so they werent soft.

Thank you for such a lovely soft meal. I am 104 and it was delicous. Unfortunitelty later that day poor Bessie slipped and smacked her chin on a metal dustbin and there was blood everywhere and Bessie screamed her head off. She had to be carted off to hospital cause her chin had got infected due to all the filth in the bin, it was overflowing with muck . A man said there was feeces in there.

 was the man right?

Thank you again for giving us the best meal of our lifes and i wish you all well at Wimpy. Perhaps you could send me a 'get well Bessie' message to give to Bessie Bates. it would really lift her spirits but you are probibly too busy with your lovly "wimpy burgers" that you make.

Thank you again for everything youve done for me and i enclose £5 for any inconveniense. We will be coming back to Wimpy as soon as we can but not with mrs Hale.

 Yours trully,

Elsie Drake

Elsie Drake (ages 104)

Thursday 29th June 2023

Dear Elsie,

It was lovely to receive your letter & positive feedback regarding your experience at one of our Wimpy restaurants. We are always happy to hear from our loyal Wimpy fans.

We were sorry to hear of Bessie's unfortunate accident and hope that she has fully recovered.

Please find enclosed your £5 note, as it really is no inconvenience to Wimpy, in fact we are thrilled that you enjoy our Wimpy Burgers.

It would be nice to know which Wimpy branch you visit so that we can forward your compliments to staff and the franchisee.

"Get well soon" Bessie, from all at Wimpy UK.

Yours sincerely

Customer Services
WIMPY UK

"Customer services"
Wimpy Burgers Restarunts
2,The Listons,
Liston Road.
  Marlow
  ;SL71FD;

July 7nd, 2023

Dear   Customor Services in Wimpy Burgers,

Thank you very much for your wonderful letter and Bessie was also happy to read your beautifull get well message, it really perked her up and she was soon able to eat her apple . She has also stopped screaming .

You asked which Wimpy Burgers did we go to? The answer was ; in London town.

I think you will be ex-cited to hear that since my last visit   I have been making some new Wimpy Burgers menus to make "Wimpy" even more delicious for everyone. It has the tipe of food I would like to see in your Wimpies.\

Mr Rudley made 50 copies on his machine, and then I put them in shops windows and on cars.   Its great advertising for Wimpy dont you think? Of course it is tiring work but someone has to do it . Bessie helped a little but had to stop as she has very brittle wrists despite her girth . We will be making lots more to put up all over the place .

I am kindly sending you one of the menus which i hope you like. Will you put them up in your Wimpy shops so me and Bessie can see them when we come to eat your delicious food? Our fame will know no end .

Thank you again, and i enclose £10 this time , since Bessie also wanted to send you five pounds so that we were the same.

Yours trully,

Elsie   Drake   (aged 104)

WIMPY **WIMPY**

NEW MENU BY
ELSIE for Summer 2023

Wimpy Beef Burge	£1
Chips	£1.10p
Wimpy Beef and kidney Burge	£1 (NEW)
Chips with kidney peices	£1.90p (NEW)
Kidney "Hot-pot"	£4.00p
Double kidney "Hot-pot"	£9.00p
Wimpy Beef, kidney and liver Burge	£1 (NEW)
Wimpy Water	NO CHARGE
~~Wimpy Egg sandwich (bun bread is used)~~	~~£0.40p~~
Cola	NO CHARGE

"Wimpy approved menu"

WIMP

Thursday 20th July 2023

Dear Elsie,

It was lovely to hear from you again and to receive your menu, you have some great ideas.

Unfortunately, we cannot put any menus up in shops or cars as they need to go through the correct procedures with our marketing team.

Please find enclosed your £10 note, please do not send any money as we cannot accept this and will have to give it to a chosen charity if you continue to do so.

Yours sincerely

Customer Services
WIMPY UK

Customer service
Wimpy burgers Restaraunts;';
  2, Teh Listons,
Liston Road, Marlow
SL7, 1FD

Elsie Drake
Granville Gardens
Lodnon

July, 27 July 2023

Dear Customer services from Wimpy,

Thank you for your kind letter and i am so glad you liked the new menus. will you be using them in the Wimpies ?

i am sure you will be happy to know   that me and Bessie made our own Wimpy burgers recently . we did them with ample kidney and mince and bulked them up with spagetti and old bread that Bessie was other-wise going to throw out. the bun we made from bread that wasnt old which we then buttered .

  Well the wimpies   were so delisious that last sunday we sold some of them in bessies garden. We laid them all out on a littel table   and everyone was excited to taste a new "Wimpy burger". in the end we raised £8 for Wimpy which is a real achievment.

Margaret took a photo of our littel table on which we showed off the new burgers . Margaret is bessies daughter but not her real one. She made the photo come out of her beautiful computor and   i am en-closing the picture here.,

  Once again this is fantatsic advertising for Wimpy and we will be doing lots more of our special "Elsies Wimpy shows" with our gorgeous table .

I am enclosing the £8 for wimpy we made. Hopefully we will make some more mony for you at our next Wimpy show in september. Will you be able to provide some wimpy hats for us to use? Bessies head is size "extra large".

Thank you   for your kindness and for offic-ially letting us sell the new lovly Wimpy burgers.

Yours trully,

Elsie Drake (aged 104)

ELSIE IS WAITING . . .

Mrs Liz Evans,
the head of Asda Supermarkets,,
  Asda house,
Great wilson Street, street
Leeds, post code: LS11,5Ad

Elsie Drake
Granville Gardens
Lodnon

July 14, July 2023'

Dear Mrs Evans,

  I am named Elsie Drake and I am 104 and the sixth oldest woman in Britin. I find it hard sometimes to write on the computor so please be patient with me kj2t122kjk\]slkcdhu'lkiy7t1'f.

  I have never shopped at Asda in my life but my friend Violet Crub told me it is very nice . They have everything there she said. Mrs Crub bought some butter and sugar and some little cakes called "Belvins" I think . They were delicious, have you eaten Belvins?

madam, I am keen to try out a Asda but am obviously very nervous cause i have never stepped foot in one before. Is it like a normal shop? Are there bells ? What i have done is write down all the things I need in Asda on a shopping list . Could you please have a look at it and tell me what you have , that way when i go to Asda I will be all nice and ready .

they might have been called "Velbins".

  Mrs Hale says she doesnt bring lists with her when she does her shoppinf as her memory is "like a rock" , but dont believe her. Yesterday she forgot to drink any water. She looked grey.

i am 104 and i would like to try a Asda please.   I enclose £5 for all your kind help in this delicate matter.

  Yours trully ,

Elsie Drake

Elsie Drake (aged 104)

<u>Elvis List for Asda</u>
(please return)

Eggs
Milk prisins?
Toothpaste
Nosepaste
Meat (I need 4 batches)
Toilet rags
food for "Potsy"
Orange squash
Belvis or "Velbins"?
Spray for tongues.
Sugar
biscuits for Cissy
stuff for Bessies feet
Clechops (I need 6 clechops)
Soap bars (40)

Mrs Elsie Drake
Granville Gardens
London

27/07/2023

Dear Elsie

Thank you for your letter. I am from the Executive Relations Team at Asda.

I have to agree with Violet, we are very nice at Asda. Unfortunately, I can't say I have heard of Belvins before, but if you pop down to your local Asda, one of our helpful colleagues will be able to provide some support in finding the product you are referring to and assist you as much as possible to ensure you have an enjoyable experience at Asda.

I have included your shopping list as well as the money you had sent within this letter.

Take care and enjoy your day, Elsie.

Kind Regards

Executive Relations Team

The managing directer of
"Land Rover Cars "
Abbey road
   whitley. ,
Coventry
CV3 4IF

Elsie Drake
Granville Gardens
Lodnon

The date is 2023

Dear managing director,

My name is Elsie Drake and I am 104 years old and the sixth oldest woman in ingland. I am learning to write on my "computor machine" , but it keeps over-heating and burning my fists.

   I am writing to you about an incredible story about one of your beautifull Land-Rover cars that i think you will like to hear.

In 1949 my husband Sidney was driving us in our "austin " brown car down down a quiet country lane when sudenly a magnificent "Land rover" car came round the corner and crashed into us. Luckily we were alright   but we couldnt believe it ; it was the Kings car! King George the 6.

   the King was not hurt apart from cuts to his eyes and mouth, but he was very very angry and started kicking our car. He kicked a window in and even spat on the bonet. Well,   my Sidney always had a terible temper but he didnt do anything and just bit his lips;   aftrer all, it was the blessed monach. Finally the king calmed down and gave Sidney a gold coin, and me sevral kisses on my cheeks and neck.

   Then King George asked us to travel with him in his Landrover for a while.   It was the nicest car ive ever been in. It even had a sort of toilet. While we were driven up and down the country lanes , the kind King sang to us for an hour. He had a gorgeous voice and i shall never forget his rendition of 'A Penny for a Pie',   although he could not do the high notes they were all flat.

When we got out the car, his driver told us never to tell any one what hapened otherwise it was "treason",   so this is the very first time i have ever told anyone this incredibal story as I did not want to hang. God save the King!

Thank you Land Rover motor-cars for letting me finally tell the truth. I just   pray i will not be hanged.

will you print my letter in your "newsletter?" Do you do newsletters at land Rover? Please let me know.   I have other stories about Land Rovers as wel if you want to hear theml, such as when Charlie Chaplin drove over my feet.   i am 104   and i like all cars.

I enclose £5 for your over-heads such as cleaning up the mucky oil.

Yours trully,

Elsie Drake

Elsie Drake (aged 104.)

Dear Elsie,

Thank you so much for taking the time to write to me and for sharing such wonderful memories. It sounds like you have led a truly exceptional life and I'm delighted that you are still taking on new challenges, even if technology can always find ways to confuse us all!

I have been lucky enough to be invited to an evening reception at Buckingham Palace next month and if the opportunity arises, I will share with His Majesty your lovely story about meeting his great-grandfather. Of course, I'll be sure not to mention you or your late husband Sidney, but it is such a special memory, I think that he'd be delighted to hear it.

I will also share your story with our Internal Communications team. We have lots of different ways to reach our many employees around the world and I'm sure that the team will be thrilled to include it in our various emails or newsletters.

I've enclosed your £5.00, which is very much appreciated but I have spoken with our Chief Finance Director and he's happy that we cover the costs, if there were any!

Thank you again for writing to me, receiving letters such as yours really makes my day.

With very warm regards,

Adrian Mardell
Chief Executive Officer

The manager of UK Athletics
UK Athletics ltd,
Alexander stadium
Walsall road, Perry Barr
Birmingham B42 2be

Elsie Drake
Granville Gardens
Lodnon

4 July in 2023.

Dear Mr Manager,

i love my hedge-hog which is called "Potsy" , and I am 104 and my name is Elsie Drake and i am the sixth oldest woman in Britian. Potsy is my hedge-hog.

I am computoring this letter to you because i need some help from athletics peoples . i am trying to organise a lovly hedge-hog race for Potsy against all the other hedg-hogs but i only have one hedge-hog, which is Potsy.   Potsy is lonly because he is practising all on his own but luckily he is getting quite fast,   cause as soon as Mrs Hale sounds the siren the noise propels him down the garden.

Athletics manager, If we cant find any other hedge-hogs for the special race, do you think   I can maybe race Potsy against rats? There are rats in the garden and Mrs Hale trapped one in a watering can on Sunday. It can't get out. Should we race "Potsy hedge-hog" against the rat? although it does seems quite an angry rat . Or what about birds? but they will probibly fly away and not bother running.

please can you help answer all my questions. i am very worried about the "Race against Potsy" event on November 5th. We have no other hedge-hogs for Potsy to race against. Bessie bates said that you train animals as well as peoples in athletics. Is this true ? do you do hedge-hogs also?   if so could you lend me some? I will pay you well for the rent of the hogs.

I am sending you £5 for your help and kindness .I pray that I hear back from you. Potsy is so sad. you can see him in my drawing I did but please can i have it back?

Yours trully,

Elsie Drake

Elsie Drake (aged 104))

Please help
"Potsy" find
some hedge-hog
friends

The RACE IS ON
BUT WHO WILL
WIN?

Bird – but it
would just fly

"Potsy"
hedge-hog

watering can

Starter
flag

Rat

Dear Elsie

  Thankyou for your wonderful letter telling us about your race against Patsy in November. —

I'm sorry we do not train animals - only human athletes but please accept our Little Brit Bear mascot and we hope he will bring you joy.

I've enclosed your £5 and your picture.   **with compliments**

       Love from UK Athletics

UKA UNITED KINGDOM ATHLETICS   BRITISH ATHLETICS   #REPRESENT

NO MORE LETTERS

Mr Dave Jones ,
The Manager
Walkers Crisps .,
450. South Oak Way,,
green Park, Reading.
RG2, 6uW

Elsie Drake
Granville Gardens
Lodnon

August 288, 2023

Dear manager of Crisps,

I am very pleased to write to you cause I am called Elsie Drake and i am 104 and the sixth oldest woman in Britin. I hope you are pleased to get this computor leter from me

are you pleased ?

i am writing to say thank you for all the years i have faithfuly eaten your lovly crisps by "Walkers" . They are so crunchy and full of flavur . My favrite ones you do   are the cheese and vinegar ones.

What are your favrite crisps?

i think you should do a new television ad-vert   about "Walkers crisps" so more people can see the benefits of eating them. for example, the advert could go like this idea i had;

A lady and a man are in their bathroom which is covered in mud and filth. The man says " Why is this room is so dirty, helen?"
   Helen is his wife of 15 years. they met in Blackpool when John ,who is the man, was working for a conpany that made butter .
Helen said: "Because we have not cleaned it for 15 years, ever since we first met!"
John says "But why didnt we clean it then when we were first in love my darling ?
They then eat   some "walkers crisps" for a long time and sudenly the bathroom is spot-less. No filth can be see anywhere not even in the toilet .
Then the packet of "Crisps" talks to us, but it is really a man just dressed up as the crisps.
The Crisps man says 'Trust Walkers crisps or you will regret it."   But the man is actually Helens father!
   Helen says "thank you father", but her father says nothing as this would mean the people watching   will know he is not really the crisps .

Do you like my idea ? Will you make this "advert"? If you do, all I would ask for is some more bags   of your beatiful crisps. Please will you let me know as i am 104 .

Thank you for all the kindess you have shown me and I enclose five pound.

Yours trully,

Elsie Drake

Elsie Drake (aged 104)

September 2023

Mrs Elsie Drake
Granville Gardens
London

Dear Mrs Drake

How lovely it is to hear from you Elsie.

Huge congratulations on enjoying our Walkers Crisps for a very long time, you may just be our oldest fan!

I have enclosed the money you sent to us as we cannot accept this. But what we can do is acknowledge your love of our great tasting crisps and would like to present you with the enclosed certificate with our compliments.

We've also enclosed a few bags of our Walkers Salt & Vinegar and Walkers Cheese & Onion crisps to enjoy a snack on us.

Thank you also for your advert idea, it raised some smiles in the office here.

Take care Elsie.

Yours sincerely

Nicola
Contact Manager
UK & Ireland Consumer Experience

Enclosure:
Certificate

Certificate of Appreciation

Thank you for being one of our oldest fans!
Your loyalty to our brand is really appreciated,

Elsie Drake

September 2023

GLOBAL
CONSUMER
EXPERIENCE Insights

WALKERS

Nicola ,
Contact mannager
Walkers Crisps;
450. South Oak way ?
Green Park Reading
   RG2 6Uw

Elsie Drake
Granville Gardens
Lodnon

22 '" september 2023

Dear Nicola,

Thank you so much for writing back to me .You are a kind lady and it is
Elsie here who is 104 .

   I also want to thank you for sending me some lovly bags of your delicious
Walkers crisps , and the special kind "serificate" that says how well I have
done for eating walkers crisps for all these years. I cannot tell you how
delighted I was , but i can really because i was very delighted !   kjhs['s;

Well i have been tucking into your crisps day and night. They are so tasty.
I even let Mrs Hale have half a bag . Bessie Bates had three bags and i also
sent a bag to my friend Violet Crub   in hospital, as she was bitten by her
gardener.   It was terible .

   Madam, eating   your crisps gave me a wonderful idea; i decided to
make my own bag of crisps. Why cant i make crisps? Im allowed arent i?

Bessie helped me and the the flavour crisps we chose was ""liver" . We
rubbed liver paste on the potato slices before we put them in the micro-
wave and they came out beautiful, only a few of them were bad.

i also designed the crisps bag but sadly Im not as good at drawing as
when I was a littel girl. I just cant get sufficient purchase on my pen, but I
tried my best madam. Elsie always tries her best .

   I hope you and your lovly Walkers staff enjoy "Elsies crisps"   which i
have enclosed in a littel platic tub. Will you be going into production with
them ? I do hope so ; my fame would know no end. I would be an icon for
my age. I am 104.

Yours truly,

Elsie Drake

Elsie Drake   (ages 104.)

Ps I am also sending you ten pound as payment.

5 October 2023
Mrs Elsie Drake
Granville Gardens
London

Dear Elsie

Hello again. I hope you are well.

I have enclosed the money you sent to us as we aren't allowed to accept money from consumers, I've also enclosed your tub as requested.

I'm really pleased that you were able to share some of your favourite crisps with your friends and also hope that Violet Crub is now on the mend after her bite.

My team thought your crisps looked great but if I'm honest Elsie I am not sure this flavour would be a big hit with our other consumers.

Adding new flavours to our current range is always a really difficult decision and one that our Marketing Development Teams and their agencies face every day. They understand that everyone has their own individual ideas and unique taste buds, giving endless choices and combinations of flavours!!

But rest assured Elsie, one thing you can rely on is that we will always do our absolute best to bring you a wide variety of amazingly tasty, top quality products that are hard to resist.

Take care and thanks again for writing.

Yours sincerely

Nicola
Contact Manager
Consumer Experience UK & Ireland

Enclosure:
Plastic tub

The editor of
Toy world magazine
61, maxted Road
"hemel Hempstead" in Hert-fordshire.
Hp2,   7PZ

Elsie Drake
Granville Gardens
Lodnon

on September 16; 2023

Dear Editor of the magazine,

My name is Elsie Drake and i am 104 years old and the sixth oldest woman in the united kingdom of Britin. My great grandson nicholas told me your magazine "Toys world" was all about toys in the world and   i am happy to make your aquantance. hello, I am elsie.

I think your wonderful readers might like to know that when my husband Sidney was alive he was very good with his hand and   he used to make littel toys out of wood and "brick and brack" and hand them out to the children in our street on Maudy thursday .

Sidneys favourite toy he made was called "McThompson " . Mcthompson was such a jaunty litle fellow, everyone lovd him.   His second favrite was a naughty squirel called "Flilton Fluffs " . McThomson and Flilton Fluffs became best friends and had many adventures for example:

- Escaping from cave
. Measles epidemic
Flood in horribel hotel
-Late for train
- The wrong wedding

Unfortinely i dont have any Mcthompons or flilton Fluffs to show you but a few months ago I decided to recreate Mcthompon and Flilton Fluffs and make them as littel toys again to glorify Sidneys blessed memory.

i wonder if your readers would be interested to see McThompson and Flilton fluffs? I would be happy to send you them to have a look. It would be a dream come true to have McThompson and Fliton Fluffs printed in your nice magzine.

i enclose £5 for all the problems i have made. please let me have my chance to shine.

Yours trully,

Elsie Drake (aged 104.)

The business magazine with a passion for toys

10th October 2023

Dear Elsie,

Thank you so much for your lovely letter. We were very interested to hear about the toys that your husband Sidney used to make himself. They sound wonderful, and how nice that he gave them out to children. They must have been delighted!

We'd love to see a picture of little McThompson and Flilton Fluffs if you have one; I'm sure our readers would be very interested. We hope to feature them in our magazine, and it would be a nice little mention for our December/Christmas edition.

I hope that's OK and look forward to hearing from you. I have returned your £5 as you have not created any problems whatsoever and it is not necessary, although it was a very kind thought.

I have noted your address and will make sure you receive a copy of the magazine if this goes ahead, which I very much hope it will, so that you can see 'your chance to shine'.

I look forward to hearing from you.

Kind Regards,

Anita Baulch
Director
Alakat Publishing – Toy World/Licensing.biz

Anita Baulch .,
the editor of,
Toy World magazine ;
61 Maxted Road in
"hemel Hempstead"
   Hertfordshirre.
HP2, 7PZ

Elsie Drake
Granville Gardens
Lodnon

October ; 17, 17 2023

Dear Anita Baulch,

   thank you very much for your lovly letter you wrote to me Elsie Drake of Britin after i wrote to you all about my littel toys i have made .

   I was so happy you want to put a picture of McThompson and Flilton Fluffs squirel in your wonderful magazine. i cannot wait for the day it comes in the shop. i will be famous , maybe even a household name ?

so I am sending you a nice photo-graph of my two toy friends together. Unfortunitly I could not operate the "email system"   and Nicolas was unable to assist as he is now in Trinidad looking at eyes cause he is an optician.

   I pray that everyone will get great pleasure looking at Mcthompson who is on the left and Flilton Fluffs on the right. A good game for your readers to play is to imagine how Mcthompson and Flilton Fluffs first met; Mcthompson was very sad   one day because someone had stolen his shoes. McThompson screamed and screamed so much that his shoes were finally returned to him by a naughty squirel called "Flilton Fluffs " .

   Whether Fliton fluffs was the one that stole Mcthomsons shoes, we may never know, but they soon became best friends and had exciting adventures, including "rocket launch".

Thank you for all your kindness you have shown me, "Toy World magazine" and i am sorry for all my computor mistakes. I enclose five pounds.

   Yours trully,

Elsie Drake

Elsie Drake (age 104)

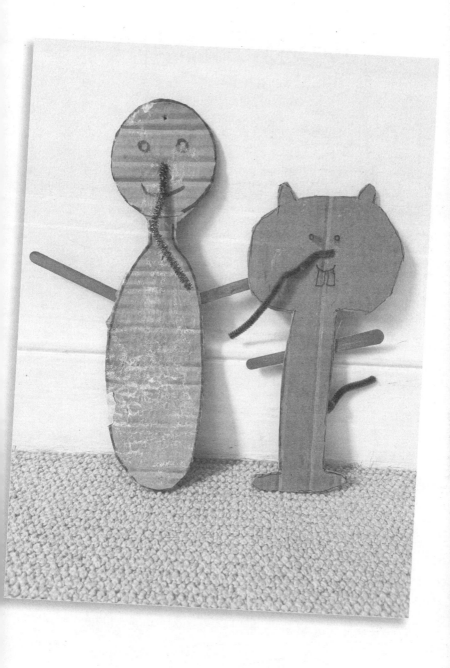

Has Toy World found its oldest reader?

The Toy World team was recently delighted to hear from a very special reader: 104-year-old Elsie Drake, from London.

After her great-grandson, Nicholas, told Elsie about Toy World, she wrote in to tell us about her beloved late husband, Sidney, who used to craft his own unique toys and hand them out every Maundy Thursday for the local children to play with.

"Sidney's favourite toy was called McThompson, who was a very jaunty fellow and loved by all," Elsie explained. "His second favourite was a naughty squirrel called Flilton Fluffs. McThompson and Flilton Fluffs became best friends and went on many adventures together, including escaping from a cave, being late for an important train, turning up at the wrong wedding and staying in hotel that ended up flooding. They even went on a rocket launch. As for how they met, well: McThompson was very upset one day because his shoes were missing, and he made such a fuss that they were ultimately returned by a naughty squirrel – and that squirrel was Flilton Fluffs."

Elsie was kind enough to include a small photograph of McThompson and Flilton Fluffs, which sadly we were unable to print in a resolution that would do them justice. Instead, we've taken the liberty of recreating their designs so that Elsie can share Sidney's creations with all the readers of Toy World.

It just goes to show – you are never too old to still enjoy toys.

McThompson

Flilton Fluffs

Mr Andrew lloyd – webber ,
the Realy Useful theater group company .
6 , Catherine street .
London town
wc2B 6JY

Elsie Drake
Granville Gardens
Lodnon

September 17; 2023,

Dear Andrew lloyd-Webber ,

My name is Elsie Drake and i am 104 and the sixth oldest woman in this
country .please excuse my errors on the machine but i sometimes find it
hard to press the buttonsss .

  Sir, i think you are narvellous.   I have enjoyed all your musical shows
such as "Josephs Coat" , "Phantoms in the opera" , "Jesus is the star" and
"Cat". They have brought me and every one else who saw them such joy.
Once a lady next to me cheered so loudly it burst my ear drum and i had
to be seen by Dr Khartis who applied linament.

  Mr Webber , when i was a young girl my sweet mother took me to see a
theater show called "Baby and Bear". Do you remember it ? it was a baby
and a bear who performed songs , well the baby sung while the bear
danced and threw things about such as tabels and chairs. No one was
injured , mind, because of the metal fences at the front and the harpoon .

It was so funny. Baby was my favrite cause he used to feed the bear small
pieces of fish from his mouth into bears mouth . baby was never atacked.

  Mr Lloyd , why dont you bring back "Baby and Bear"? i think it would be a
great hit,   and it would be my dream to relieve my childhood watching baby
and bear break things again on stage, while your beautiful songs played
loudly through the speakers . You could even sell fish-scraps in the theater for
the people to throw at the bear , although their hands might get a bit smelly.

soapy water in plastic bowls under the seats ?

Do you think you will make "Baby and Bear " ? I am sending you five
pound to help you make it for me as well as a poster you could use when
you do the show.

I am 104 and want to see the antics of baby and his angry bear before I "go".

Yours trully,

Elsie Drake

Elsie Drake (aged, 104)

"Baby and Bear"
by Andrew Lloyd Webber

on-Stage

Watch
Baby
feed Bear
fish from
his mouth

Bear
is
always
angry

Elvie

THE REALLY USEFUL GROUP LIMITED

From the office of Andrew Lloyd Webber

Wednesday 20th September 2023

Dear Mrs Drake,

Thank you so much for your kind letter to Lord Lloyd Webber.

It was so lovely to read about how much you enjoy Lord Lloyd Webber's productions. Thank you for the wonderful poster you have designed for 'Baby and Bear'.

I'm sure you can imagine that due to the amount of letters and emails that Lord Lloyd Webber receives daily from all over the world, unfortunately Lord Lloyd Webber won't be able to respond personally. We are therefore returning the money you kindly sent us.

Thank you again for taking the time to write to him.

Best wishes,

Elysia Moseley
Personal Assistant to Andrew Lloyd Webber

Elysia moseley,
Peronel asistant to Mr Andrew Lloyd -Webber ,
   The Really Usful Theater Group company ;
6 ,Catherine Street .
London town WC2B 6Jy

Elsie Drake
Granville Gardens
Lodnon

On October 3, 2023;

Dear Elysia Moseley,

Thank you for your kind letter you sent to me, Mrs Elsie drake who is 104 all about the "Baby and Bear" show. It was a lovly letter and it warmed my hearts no end. Thank you for all your kindness, madam.

Unfortunitly you did not say if you are actualy interested in making "Baby and Bear " because if you are then i would be happy to help Mr Webber   write this wonderful show. This is the "opening song" i wrote which is sung to the tune of the "national anthem" of Britin;

God save our baby and bear,
They are nice and they dont care
      they are baby and bear.

Baby feeds bear from his mouth
when they are north or south
And when they're east or west
Baby and bear are the best!

the second song is done to the tune of "Rule Britannia". Do you know this song?

Rule Britainnia,
Baby play with bear
Bear is angry angry angry
Bear throws chair.

   Baby wears nappy
He likes to roll around,
   Baby never never never
does toilet on the ground

the third tune is mainly screaming cause Bear is very angry and baby is scared. its very funny cause baby then pushes Bear off the stage ,but will the angry bear atack the audience ?

Would Mr Webber be willing to meet me to discuss writing the musical "Baby and Bear " with me? i do hope so. I am 104 with a sertificate from the queen on my wall.

Please give me a chance to astonish the world. I enclose five pound English monies.

Yours trully,

Elsie Drake (aged; 104

THE REALLY USEFUL GROUP LIMITED

From the office of Andrew Lloyd Webber

Friday 13th October 2023

Dear Mrs Drake,

Thank you for responding to my previous letter.

I have enclosed the money you kindly sent to put towards the idea of Baby and Bear.

For legal reasons it is not possible for Lord Lloyd Webber to review unsolicited material / ideas personally. As a company we have always received a great deal of unsolicited work and many ideas for new musicals, songs and projects. Sadly, we are returning your idea unseen, read or heard by Lord Lloyd Webber.

It was most kind of you to share your enthusiasm and passion for Andrew's work and I am so sorry to have to send you this disappointing reply.

Thank you again for taking the time to write to him.

Best wishes,

Elysia Moseley
Personal Assistant to Andrew Lloyd Webber

The manager of ;
Victoria and Alberts   museum
Crom-well road,
London
london
london SW7 2rL

Elsie Drake
Granville Gardens
Lodnon

19 in September in 2023

Dear the Manager of Victoria and alberts museem,

My name is Elsie drake and I am 104   years of age and and i am also the
sixth oldest woman in Britin . I have seen so many things in my life; ;

  birds, horribel fighting, different coins being made .

Can you help me please sir? i know that you know everything about our
blessed Queen victoria so i am hoping you can assist me.

  Last week Mrs hale told me that Queen victoria is still alive and that she
never died and that you are keeping her in the basement of Victoria and
Alberts museum.   i said "Of course she is dead, she drowned   a hundred
years ago." Mrs hale said "Its not rubbish elsie they are keeping her alive
by feeding her a special tipe of liquid. She will be unveiled in ten years
time by King charles. " rubbish Mrs Hale :"it is not" "Yes! " "No Elsie" "It is"
"Dont talk dung you beast" she shouted.

i am very sorry but   i wonder if you could please help settle this terible
argument by kindly writing back to Mrs Hale and telling her she is wrong
and that you are not keeping Queen Victoria alive under your lovly
museum. Mrs Hale lives in my house so its the same adress for the letter
and stamp .

  With your kind help perhaps i shall get some piece and quiet, as Mrs
hale keeps screaming about Queen victoria drinking that liquid .

  I thank you for your generosity in dealing with this fragile matter , and
send you a nice   five pound note for my computoring mistakes . i am 104.

  Yours trully,

Elsie Drake

Elsie Drake (aged 104.)

Mrs Hale
Granville Gardens
London

10th of November 2023

Dearest Mrs Hale,

We would all like to reassure you, that we are not keeping Queen Victoria in the basement of the Victoria and Albert Museum and we are not feeding her a special type of liquid.

We hope that this has reassured you.

We wish you all the best.

Kind regards,

The Contact Center Team
Visitors Experience
The Victoria and Albert Museum

the Managing directer of
Severn house rormance Books
Eardley house
4 Uxbridge Street ;'
London W8. 7SY

Elsie Drake
Granville Gardens
Lodnon

19 in September. 2023>

Dear Manager of Severn House romantic books,

i am 104 and the sixth oldest woman in Britin and i have been reading books about love and romance   for over 80 years. My favrite one was about the Prince and his sister. was it called "The Palace of forbidden Love?.

I am writing   because i want to make a very special romantic book for your company, "Sevren House Book". its all about a gentleman I have recently met called Ralf Groberts who is ever so nice. Mr groberts is a younger man at 100 but I dont mind if people talk. However, I do hope my husband Sidney who died in 1950   is not looking down thinking "what are you doing with that man elsie? Dont touch the man" but it is all very inocent. Weve only done cuddles ,although Ralf did kiss my hands and feet once.

Ralf is a sensitive soul. He used to run a company that made hutches for turkeys. He once told me a turkey   escaped by chewing through the wire and was sadly run over by a lorry.   Ralf Groberts wept as he told me this brutal story. He is a very gentle man and I think we might even be a bit in love . Who says you cant love when youre 104 ?

mrs Hale says it.

My book will be about our lovly love and its all made up of the hundreds of romantic letters we write to each other.   It is   called "Elsie Drake and Ralf Groberts – letters of Beautifull Love". So far weve only actually written one letter each but we will definity do lots more.   I am sending you these sensual letters along with five pound monies for all your kindness.

Severn House books , i would like to make this blessed book with you so can i come in to meet you?   Please let me have my chance to shine . i am 104.

I apolo-gise for the terrible errors i have done with the computor , but i found out that mrs Hale has been pouring milk on the buttons and the smell is absolutely apaling.

Yours trully,

Elsie Drake (aged 104)

To Ralf Groberts from Elsie

october 4, 2023

Dear Ralf,

i hope you don't mind me using the computor to write to you but Nicholas said its very important i learn about the "modern world". Nicholas is my great grandson, did i tell you about him? he works with teeth cause he is a dentist by trade, no not dentist I mean optician, i cannot find the button that gets rid of the mistakes, so i had to leave the dentist bit in.

I am sorry Ralf

it was very nice to see you yesterday and nice to learn all about your life. Did you ever get bitten by your turkeys :? My friend Violet Crub told me she once got atacked by a swarm of turkeys who wuldnt stop biting her back. she was in hospital for months. There was so much pus. Poor Violet.

the man is coming round later to look for the source of the smell in my room i told you about, the eggy smell. it seems to be coming from the computor machine. it actually smells more like a filthy toilet when people havent flushed it for weeks. i remember when I worked in the amunitions factory in the war and we had to use buckets for our waste. The smell was so foul it made everyone so sick they had to keep another bucket nearby just for the vomit. it was a terible time.

Ralf groberts, i think it is almost time we did a kiss. would you like to do a kiss with me? You dont have to kiss my face, you can kiss my sweet hands to start with if you want. They are very clean. i scrub them every day with soap and hot water. i know how strongly you feel about germs on the body, Ralf.

If we do kiss then maybe we could have a small one at the beginning and then do longer ones, for example the firtst kiss could be 2 secnds, and the next one   3 seonds and so on until we do about a hundred years of kissing, no I meant a hundred seconds kissing I cant find the button.

Can we kiss for a hundred years my dear Ralph? I meant a hundred seconds again, where is the mistakes button?

do you love me Ralf Groberts?
yours trully,

Elsie

Elsie

TO ELSIE,

THANK YOU FOR YOUR LETTER.
THE SMELL DOES NOT SOUND
NICE, MAYBE IT IS RODENTS. WE
HAD RATS ON OUR FARM, THE CAT
KILLED DOZENS. OR A BIRD MIGHT
HAVE JUST DIED IN GUTTERING BY
YOUR WINDOW.

BEWARE OF MAGGOTS THOUGH.

I WILL ~~CAN~~ THINK ABOUT KISSING
YOU PERHAPS WE JUST START WITH
VERY SHORT ONES ON HANDS AS YOU
SAID BUT YOU MUST USE SOAP FIRST.
I WILL BRING A SOAP BAR FOR YOUR
HANDS. IT IS A 'MEDICATED' SOAP
BAR.

FROM, RALF.

Severn House +

CANON‖GATE

canongate.co.uk

Dear Elsie,

Thank you for your letter. I'm afraid we won't be able to take on your book proposal.

We wish you and Ralf all the best!

Kind Regards,

assistant at Severn House & Canongate

'My greatest wish —
other than salvation
— was to have a book'
Life of Pi, YANN MARTEL

NO MORE LETTERS

The Royal society of Medicine.
number 1,
wimpole Streeet;
  London
w1G 0AE

Elsie Drake
Granville Gardens
Lodnon

20, September in 2023

Dear person in charge of the Royal society of Medicines,

  My name is Elsie Drake and i am 104 years of age and also the sixth oldest woman in the land. Well done elsie .

  i am looking forward to giving my speech at the "royal Society of Medicines" on November the 23 at 7 o clock at night . It is a very famous society where men and ladies learn all about medicine, such as headache pills and creams for agony .

how long does my speech have to be? Can i read it off parchment? And what hapens if i am late? Will i be punished by doctors? How will i get there? What will i be fed ?

  But why do i have to give you all a speech? Shouldnt you be giving me a speech instead ? i dont even know about medicine .

Please can you let me know all the answers as soon as posible. Thank you for your kindness . i am 104 and i enclose £5 for your help.

Yours trully,

Elsie Drake

Elsie Drake (aged 104)

The ROYAL
SOCIETY of
MEDICINE

Patron HM The Queen

Mrs Elsie Drake
Granville Gardens
London

04 October 2023

Dear Mrs. Drake,

Thank you for your letter of the 20th September.

I'm sorry it has taken so long to reply, however we have been trying to find the event at which you have been asked to speak on the 23rd November, and we have been unable to.

Can I suggest that you contact the person who asked you to speak, or can you send their details so we can contact them to speak to you.

You may have received an invitation to attend a meeting, rather than speak at it, so I apologise if this has caused any misunderstanding.

I have enclosed and returned the £5.00 sent, help is free of charge, especially to someone who has reached such a fantastic age!

Yours Sincerely,

John Armstrong

mr John Amstrong;,
the Royal Society of Medcine,
1, Wimpole street';
   London
W1g 0AE

Elsie Drake
Granville Gardens
Lodnon

9,9 October, 2023

Dear Mr Armstrong,

It is elsie and I wrote to you all about my speech Im giving in your building on 23 November and you kindly wrote me back a sweet letter . Thank you for your grace, sir. i do not get much grace in my life. Mrs Hale has no grace at all.

You asked me if i know who told me to do the speech, well it was a man and he spoke with a very deep voice . Roger Ludby? was it? or Wilf Ludby? i am sorry but i am terible with names. Once i forgot my own name! I thought I was called "Elfie" but its "Elsie " of course. People laughed so much, i felt appaling shame .

  why did they need to laugh so much?

My speech is now coming on nicely. It is called   "Medicine we use " and its quite a long speech because theres just so much medicine in the world. Also i thought I might start by showing every one how i take my own medicine each day and how i apply my ointment to my body . Do you think people will like this idea sir ?

thank you again for your kindness and i look forward to meeting you. For your infor-mation , I will be traveling by bus on the 23rd, and my guests will be mrs Irene Nineapple and Mrs Bessie bates . Will we get dinner please? I think Bessie will need her dinner . I enclose five pound for the inconvenienses.

Yours trully

Elfie Drake

Elfie Drake (aged 104)

The ROYAL
SOCIETY of
MEDICINE

Patron HM The Queen

Mrs Elsie Drake
Granville Gardens
London

30 October 2023

Dear Mrs Drake

Thank you for your letter dated 9 October 2023 addressed to Mr John Armstrong, which has been passed to me.

I am afraid that I am having a little difficulty in finding a meeting at the Royal Society of Medicine on 23 November 2023. I have asked around various departments and officers but can find no record of an invitation being sent out.

I wonder if there might be a telephone number I can call you on to see if I can help further? Or perhaps you or one of your guests will be able to give me a call and we can sort this out.

I am also returning the £5 that you included with your letter – whilst the gesture is greatly appreciated, there is really no need to do this.

I look forward to hearing from you.

Kind regards,
Yours sincerely

Mrs Joanna Rose
Charity Secretary

Mrs Joanna Rose,
The Royal society of Medecine,
1 Wimpole Street .
London ,
W1G; 0AE

Elsie Drake
Granville Gardens
Lodnon

6. November. 2023

Dear Mrs Rose,

Thank you so much for your kind letter you wrote to my house .

I am so sorry, madam, but I got it all wrong. I am not supposed to be giving a speech at the Royal society of Medicine on November the 23rd, I am supposed to be taking my new medicine on November 23rd. It is a terible mix up and I do not know how i got it all so wrong.

I apologise greatly for all the trubbles I beset you and the other man. Elsie has been such a fool.   Can you ever forgive me the Royal Society of Medcine?

i enclose five pounds donation monies as recompense for my dredful blunder and thank you again for being such a beautiful company.

Yours trully,

Elsie Drake

Elsie Drake (age 104)

Ps The new medicine I have to take is for my noses.

137

The person in charge of
"Led by Donkeys"
  71 – 75 Shelton street
London
Wc2h 9JQ

Elsie Drake
Granville Gardens
Lodnon

Setember ,30 in 2023

Dear manager of Led by donkeys ,

   My name is Elsie Drake and im 104 years old of age and the sixth oldest
woman in this country.   i hope you do not mind me using my computor
to write to you but i am trying to "keep up with the tims ".

I am writinf to tell you that i visited your beautiful donkey sanctuary last
week and i had such a lovly day, all thanks to you. The donkeys were so
friendly and clean, there was very little muck or dung anywhere . i also
stroked about five donkeys and was not bitten once.

   When i was married, my Sidney got bitten terribly by a horribel donkey
on an illegal farm near Wimborne. It was awful, they thought Sidney
would lose his arms. Luckily he got better in the end but had to spend
two months in hopital where he had his wallet pinched by one of the
doctors, "Dr Zeff", who got sent to prison as he had also been stealing
some of the machines there too. Aparently he wanted to use them to
make powerful X-Ray wepons.

   I will never forget my day out with your glorious animals and I am
sending you a five pound note donation , perhaps you can buy the
donkeys some more hay or gruel.

   such lovly donkeys,

Thank you for everything you and your donkeys have done for me. Please
kindly let me know the mony arrived.

Yours trruly,

Elsie Drake

Elsie Drake (aged 104)

Dear Elsie

Thank you so much for your donation. Alas we are not a donkey sanctuary but are instead a political accountability campaign, so we are returning your £5. All the best!

Led By Donkeys

NO MORE LETTERS

The manager of
Blackpool Pleasure beach   theme Park.
524, ocean Boulevard
   Blackpool, FY 4 1Ez

Elsie Drake
Granville Gardens
Lodnon

9 Octoctober. 2023

Dear Manager ,

i am called Elsie Drake and I am 104 years of age and the sixth oldest
woman in Britin.   i am writinf cause I would like to start a new theme
park based inside your wonderful Blackpol pleasure Beach theme park. I
think it will be a great success, everyone will want to go , even the King
but we will have to give him a discount.

My theme park is called "Potsy Land"   and it is all about Potsy who is my
hedge-hog that lives in my garden. We have some lovly adventures
together ;for example feeding him from my hand or dancing near him. We
also play the "Potsy hide" game ; Potsy hides in the mud and I try to find
him with my stick while Mrs Hale beats her drum.

There will be rides aplenty in Potsy land, and   a special "Guess Potsys
weight machine". Theres also a chance to meet Potsy and share his food
from his bowl (if the counsil alow it), plus lots more fun for the family.

antiseptic cream

I enclose a drawing of "Potsy Land", although I will need it back as I only
have one copy cause Mr Rudleys photo-copy machine caught fire last
week . Police say that a man called "Roger Leaf" did it. Aparently hes
started a dozen fires in the past year alone. I do hope they catch him. do
you think theyll catch "Roger leaf"?

Sir or lady, please let me know when we can start building Potsy Land.
But how long do you think it will take to build? A month ? a year? twenty
years? Please can you tell me as I dont have much time cause I am 104.
Potsy is sad.

i enclose five pounds.

Yours trully,

Elsie Drake

Elsie Drake (ages 104)

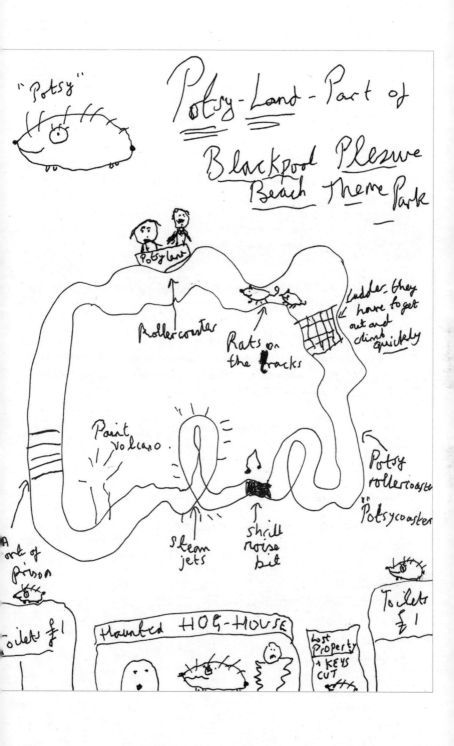

19th October, 2023

Mrs Elsie Drake
Granville Gardens
London

Dear Elsie,

Thank you very much for your letter and taking the time to design 'Potsy Land'.

Whilst we absolutely loved your idea of 'Potsy Land', unfortunately it's not something that we can implement at Blackpool Pleasure Beach. We did, however, love the idea too much to let go, so we have brought your map to life.

Please find enclosed our interpretation of your design and Potsy and his friends on a rollercoaster. We hope you like it and find it fit for our King!

Thank you for sending the five pounds, which is enclosed in this letter.

Yours sincerely,

James Cox
Director of Sales, Marketing and PR
enc

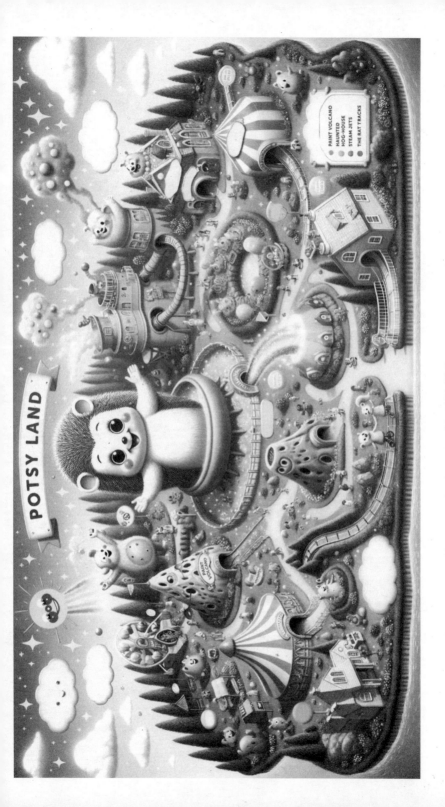

NO MORE LETTERS

the Lady or Man who is "in charge"
of
Stonehenge
Salis-bury,
Sp4, 7DE

Elsie Drake
Granville Gardens
Lodnon

Its october 12, year 2023

Dear   manager of   Stonehenge ,

i am called Elsie Drake and I am 104 years of age and the sixth oldest woman in Britin.   i am writinf to you on a computor but i do find it quite difficult to use, and i still cannot find the button for capital numbers .

Can you help me please?.   i have a sofa that is sadly haunted by a terible ghoul called "the Pink Lady". She is a lady spirit dressed from head to toes in pink who scares me no end.   She shouts horribel names at me at night such as "hog", 'slimebag" and "Lady of the latrine ", they are not nice names, not nice at all.

  My friend Bessie Bates told me   that the best way to destroy her would be to set fire to the sofa in a "sacred plaice" , so we chose Stonehenge which has all those big stones that were dumped there by cave-mean a million years ago i think.

  Bessie's   great-grandson Neville said he is happy to take us down to Stonehenge in his big van on December 1st to carry out the ghostly burning seremony. We will be ariving just after our lunch.

Sir or madam,im just checking that its alright for us to burn the cursed sofa in the middle of all the stones with parafin . Im sure it is alright though because stones cant go on fire can they?   and anyway even if all the stones do start burning up ,we will be bringing sevral ready filled buckets of water just in case.

i look forward to hearing from you otherwise we will see you in december.   i also enclose five pounds of English money for your assistance in the destruction of the wicked "Pink lady " .

Yours trully,

Elsie Drake

Elsie Drake (aged 104)

ENGLISH HERITAGE

Mrs Elsie Drake
Granville Gardens
London

Date 09/11/23

Dear Elsie,

I hope this message finds you well. Thank you for reaching out to us with your unique request. It's always interesting to hear from people who appreciate and want to engage with the site. I'm writing in response to your query about burning a haunted sofa within the boundaries of Stonehenge.

While we understand that people have a wide range of interests and ideas, we must respectfully inform you that burning any items within the Stonehenge World Heritage Site is not allowed. There are several important reasons for this restriction:

1. Preservation of Cultural and Natural Heritage: The World Heritage Landscape which Stonehenge sits within is home to a rich and diverse cultural heritage that spans across centuries. Our primary responsibility is to protect and preserve these invaluable assets for future generations.

2. Safety Concerns: Burning an item like a sofa, even if it is believed to be haunted, can pose significant safety hazards to both visitors and the environment. We must always prioritise the safety and well-being of all individuals within our site.

3. Legal and Regulatory Compliance: Stonehenge is subject to various legal regulations and guidelines. Burning objects, particularly within the context of the site, would contravene Section 19 Subsection 3f of the Stonehenge Regulations 1997, and we are committed to adhering to all applicable laws.

If you have any other questions or require assistance with planning a visit in a way that aligns with our site's policies, please do not hesitate to contact us.

Thank you for your understanding, and please find enclosed the money you sent us.

Best regards,

Richard Dewdney
Operations Manager
Stonehenge

The chairman of
the horse of The Year Show; '
Stoneleigh Park
  kenilworth
  Warwickshure ,CV8 2LZ

Elsie Drake
Granville Gardens
Lodnon

Ocober 15, 2023

Dear Chairman of the horses,

I am 104 and my name is Elsie Drake and I am the sixth oldest woman in Britin. I am writing on a computor . Do you write on computors?

The reason for my letter is that I wonder if I can come to your lovly horse show and tell the world all about my long life with beautiful horses? it would be a dream for Elsie and i will be so proud when every one calls my name. They even gave me a standing ovation.

Here are some exampals of the wonderful stories i will tell; ;

Once, during the Depression we hadnt eaten for days and we had no mony, so my father decided we would have to milk the horse. We all took turns but "Lucky" didn't mind. When the neigh-bours heard about this they milked Lucky too in exchange for "pammies" which were small cakes made from old offal . I can still remember the taste of horse milk, it was so sweet.   God rest our souls.

There used to be a horse called "Master Slump". He was a very clever animal. He could jump through hoops made of electrified copper, and if we turnd up the voltage he would jump even faster! Poor Master Slump .

These are the two horses ive known and loved, and I miss them very much .

please let me have my chance to shine, and share some of these magnificent horse tales at the world famous "Horse of The year Show". Another time Lucky sudenly ran amok on a farm and stamped five geese to death.   The honking was awful. I wont tell that story though .

I enclose five pounds for your kind help to make the celebration of "Elsie and the beautiful two horses she knew" a day I will never forget.   Will I need to bring my own micro-phone?

Yours trully,

Elsie Drake

Elsie Drake (aged 104)

Elsie Drake, Aged 104
Tells stories about beautiful
HORSES she knew
at:
"The Horse of the Year Show"

Admission £100

Horse
of the
Year
Show

Dear Elsie,

Thank you for taking the time to write to us at the Horse of the Year Show.

Plans are well underway for the show in its 75th anniversary year. And we have displays organised to showcase the versatility and grace of British-bred horses.

Alongside this we have a packed competition schedule featuring many prestigious championship finals across five days.

We love to hear people's stories about their lifetime spent with horses and ponies and the great memories they have made together.

We have sent a small memento from the HOYS office for you.

If you have access to the internet please do take a look at the Horse of the Year Show website for all the latest information.

Best wishes for your 105th birthday this year.

The HOYS Team

NO MORE LETTERS

The Chairman of ;
Wimbledon tennis match tornaments,
  the All England lawn Tennis club;;
  church Road.,
Wimbledom
  London, post code;;
SW19, 5ae

Elsie Drake
Granville Gardens
Lodnon

It is 16 of october, year; 2023

Dear chairman of Wimbledon tennis games,

  i am Elsie Drake who is 104 and also the sixth oldest woman in Britin. I am writinf to you on a "computor", because I want to keep up with the modern world . Whats wrong with keeping up with the moden world ? I ought to be allowed to, oughtend I?

Sir, this is perhaps the most dificult letter i have ever written, and one that i have been meaning to write for nearly seventy five years.   In 1949, i atended a tennis game with my late husband sidney at your wonderful Wimbledon tenis courts. i cant remember who we were watching , was it Martha Hendy and Enid Soames? Did they do tennis?   Anyway, Enid if it was her ,or martha if it was her, one of them hit the ball so hard it landed rihgt in my bag. i couldnt believe it, it was a one in a billion tennis ball shot.

Sir, i was going to throw the ball back , i swear, but instead I did a terrible thing. I slowly did my bag up when no one was looking, and took the beautiful ball home with me.   Please forgive me .

  i have never told anyone about this horrendous secret until now and it feels like an enormous weihgt has been lifted from my bosom. so i am finally returning the sacred ball back to Wimbledon, seventy five years on with this letter.

i hope to god that you and all the players of tennis in the world can forgive my retched deed , and   i enclose five pounds for any administritive costs caused by the ball, for example cleaning it.

Will the ball go in a museum? will i be famous? Please will you let me know that the ball arived with you safely,   and i apologise again for my wicked crime.

  Yours trully,

Elsie Drake

Elsie Drake (aged 104.)

Mrs Elsie Drake
Granville Gardens
London

10 November 2023

Dear Elsie

Your visit to Wimbledon in 1949

Thank you so much for your recent letter in which you detailed the events that took place during your visit to The Championships in 1949. It is truly amazing that memories of your day at Wimbledon remain so vivid after all this time.

And so to the incident that sparked your letter. Whilst we obviously encourage any balls that leave the court during play to be returned, I think we all understand the temptation that exists when one falls into your hands (or more literally on this occasion into your bag). I am sorry that you have lived with a feeling of guilt for such a long period of time, but can only admire your desire to set the record straight and return the ball in question. I am sure my predecessor colleagues would have been happy to forgive you for this spontaneous act and would have been delighted to receive your letter of contrition.

In your letter you asked if we could confirm safe receipt of the ball. Whilst I can confirm that your letter arrived safe and sound, we were somewhat surprised at the enclosure, which proved to be a slipper, rather than the ball you clearly intended to return. We are therefore returning it to you – along with some other (more recent) Wimbledon keepsakes to add to your collection – as we suspect you will need your slippers as we head into Winter.

Finally, it is great to see that you are keeping up with the modern world and I hope we can put on a fantastic Championships for your 105th year!

Very best regards
Yours sincerely

Michelle Dite
Operations Director

NO MORE LETTERS

The leader of the
  London Philharmonic Orcestra, ,
16, Clerkenwell Green
  london EC1r 0QTp?

Elsie Drake
Granville Gardens
Lodnon

October month 19 day; 2023, year

Dear Leader ,

  My name is Mrs. Elsie Drake and   I am 104 and also the sixth oldest
woman in great Britin. Sir or lady, It has always been my dream to play in
the London philharmomic orchestra , which is known all over the world
for its beautiful music it does

  Batehoven

So can i join your orchestra then ? i think I will be a very good addition as
I can play the penny whistle to a proficient standard . For exampel i can
play "The Busmans Friend" quite nicely and quite loudly, although Mrs
Hale says that i sound like a "dying bird". But do not listen to her cause her
piano playing sounds worse than a screaming man.

  I think people will appreciate seeing an older lady playing with your
orcestra, it will be a talking point, everyone will flock to the theaters when
Elsie is blowing into her pipe. I may be 104, but I still feel as young as i did
when i was a littel girl living in whitechapel, playing my whistle in the
road and chasing rats with my pole.

  i look forward to seeing you in your office on December the 1st   cause i
will be nearby that day, as I have to see an expert about   my nose. I
promise to bring my penny whistle and i will play my littel heart out for
you.

  Thank you for your grace and   I enclose   five pounds to help me get in
to your glorious orchestra

  Yours trully ,

Elsie Drake

Elsie Drake (age 104.)

London **Philharmonic** Orchestra

Mrs Elsie Drake
Granville Gardens
London

17 November 2023

Dear Elsie,

I write in reply to your lovely letter, dated 19 October, that reached us rather later than you had perhaps intended.

Your kind words and donation of £5 was initially sent to the Royal Philharmonic Orchestra who are based at Clerkenwell Green – we are very much south of the river, residing in Vauxhall.

We were touched by your kind words about the Orchestra and honoured to have received a letter from the sixth oldest woman in Great Britain!

I am afraid that we're not currently in need of a penny whistle-player but should a programme of repertoire arise that calls for such an addition, we will absolutely keep you in mind!

I do hope that you and Mrs Hale can set aside your musical differences, perhaps there's a duet to be played.

Once again, thank you for sending your gift to the Orchestra which we are very grateful for.

With all best wishes

Rosie Morden
Individual Giving Manager

Rosie Morden
   Individual giving maanager .
the   London philharmonic Orcestra
89 Albert embankment;'
london se17,tp

Elsie Drake
Granville Gardens
Lodnon

25 of november of 2023

Dear Rosie Morden,

  It is Elsie again. Thank you for your respectful letter which i read in my chair.

  It is a shame you do not need a penny whistle blower in your orcestra, however Mrs Hale and i have taken your lovly advice and been practising together all day long. The problum is she keeps playing the wrong notes but saying its my fault.

  "Elsie stop playing all those terible notes" she shouted "im not playing terrible notes Mrs Hale, im blowing my whistle quite properly thank you." "Well you sound like a dustbin lorry" "no i do not, youre the one hammering the piano with her fists" "How dare you? Im using my fingers very delicitly you dung" she screamed. it was a horribel argument. Later, i put flour in her bed.

Madam, when we get abit better perhaps Mrs Hale and i could become a sort of "supporting act" to your orcestra. Maybe we could do our piano and whistle duetts in in the middle bit of the concert, when people go off to use toilets .

  perhaps you could give us a special "audition" like on the televison. But what will the prize be? a holiday? a thousand pounds? cars? I think I will choose the holiday but i will be not be going on a plane with Mrs Hale again. The last time we went she was a beast to the pilot. He was crying. We all were.

  I think we will be ready for our audition on February 1st, But i will need to book my travel tickets for then, so can you please confirm this date as we will need to practse every single day. It is very tiring work, i am exausted.

i enclose ten pounds costs.

Yours trully

Elsie Drake

Elsie Drake (aged 104)

London **Philharmonic** Orchestra

Mrs Elsie Drake
Granville Gardens
London

11 December 2023

Dear Mrs Drake

I write in reply to your letter dated 25 November.

We are very grateful for your enthusiasm for the London Philharmonic
Orchestra however I am afraid that we are not able to hear an audition from
you, nor are we in a position to programme any sort of performance. As such
I am returning the £10 that you sent along with your letter.

On behalf of everyone here, we wish you all the very best with your playing
and a happy and music-filled 2024.

Best wishes

Rosie Morden
Individual Giving Manager

His holynness the Pope
The Vatican
Vatican Town Hall
Italy country

Elsie Drake
Granville Gardens
Lodnon

October 29,,, 2023

Dear Mr Pope,

  My name is Elsie Drake and I am 104 years old and the sixth oldest woman in Britin. I am writinf this on a computor which is connected to a box which will print my later for me letter on.

  The Pope, at brekfast this morning,, Mrs Hale told me that you have the power to fly and also to burn holes in metal objects just by looking at them,. I told her that this was not true so she took away my food items and buried them in the garden.

  where is the justice in the world?

Will you plesase write back to me on your holy computor and say that you cannot fly or burn holes in metal objecs just by looking at them? That way I can show horribel Mrs hale your letter and she wil have to retreive my food items and I can then have my lovly breakfast.

please help little Elsie. I enclose £5 money as well as a picture of you flapping about and burning things.

Yours trully,

Elsie Drake

Elsie Drake (aged 104)

PS if you can actually fly and burn holes in metel then please just pretend you cant. it will be our little secret, sire.

The Flying Pope burning a hole
in a metal lorry

by
Elsie
Drake
aged 10¼

Pope

lorry

SEGRETERIA
PER L'ECONOMIA

From the Vatican, 4 December 2023

Dear Mrs Drake,

The Secretariat for the Economy has been asked by His Holiness to express his gratitude for the offering of £ 5.00, sent to him and for the sentiments the prompted this charitable gift.

Yours sincerely,

Fr. Raffaele Lanzilli, S.I.
Secretary of the Prefect

NO MORE LETTERS

The person who runs
  the "House of Marbles shop" shop
The Old pottery ;'
p ottery Road '
  Bovey Tracey.
Newton abbot
TQ13 9dS

Elsie Drake
Granville Gardens
Lodnon

3 November., 2023

Dear House of Marbles shop manager,

I am called Elsie Drake who is 104 and the sixth oldest woman in Britin, Thank you for letting me write to you on my computor. it comes with a screen and everyday it shows me all the infomation i need. Yesterdays infomation was "Colchester" .

i have always loved marbles and i remembver   the first time I visited your world famous wonderful marbles shop to buy marbles back in 1975. Everyone was so kind to me. A man even kissed me but i didnt mind. It was such a gentle kiss.

Marbles shop owners, I am writing to ask if you can help me solve a marbles mystery   that   has haunted me my whole life;

  How do they put the coloured bits in the middle of the marbles ? i have never known the truth to this terible secret. Bessie said they just grow the glass around the bit in the middle,   but how do you grow glass? and what exacly is in the middle of all the littel marbles?   Mrs hale said that the stuff in the middle is just seeds, except if its   green, cause thats a pea

Is it peas?

Thank you for your help in this awful matter. i do hope you can put my sweet mind at rest, i cant sleep at night for thinking about the poor marbles . I enclose five pound for all your good help and send you my blessings. i am 104.

Yours trully,,

Elsie Drake (aged 104.)

7th November 2023

Mrs Elsie Drake
Granville Gardens
London

Dear Mrs Drake,

Thank you very much for your letter and your enquiry into how marbles are made. It's no wonder you're curious as it's a very exciting process!

Colour is added to liquid/molten glass, this then moves to a tank from which small globs of glass are released and then cut to size. The small globs of glass then roll down ramps and into grooved metal rollers that create spheres from the globs and subsequently cool the molten glass. After they have completely cooled down, they are then sorted and packaged – and voila you have marbles!

Whilst we appreciate your offer of five pounds it is truly not needed, so please find it enclosed with this letter.

We do hope you are no longer haunted by the mystery of marble making!

Yours sincerely,

House of Marbles

NO MORE LETTERS

The Chairman
England Rugby
that does the English rugby team,
twickenham Stadium
200, Whitton road [
  Twickenham ; Middle-sex
  tw2, 7BA

Elsie Drake
Granville Gardens
Lodnon

4, November month , 2023

Dear Chairman of the rugby,

Good day to you sir and   my name is Elsie Drake and im 104 years old of age and the sixth oldest woman in Britin. This letter is being done on my "computor" . Electrisity is inside it all the time.

  I want to thank you and the wonderful English rugby team for all your success in the rugby world cup competition that you played rugby in. I watched it with my friend Bessie Bates, and even Potsy hedge-hog sat and watched while he ate his grubs.

Sir. it would be my dream if you could kindly thank all the players in your lovly team for bringing me such joy.

  So Elsie thanks;   Peter shill, Oliver Penhaligon,   clive Marsh,, 'Flum' the captain, Norbert Glove, the Lewis twins, Ian Theogmorton, Ben Tenlt, Paul Pinny and   David Lime,   I am very sorry if I missed any of your players off my gorgeous list. i do hope I have not upset any of the men.

I am enclosing five pounds, so please buy the men something nice. i am sorry its not more money but i do not have much cause i am 104 and keep making mis-takes on the computor. Sometimes Mrs hale puts glue on the buttons.

  Please let me know if the men are happy with my letter or if i have angered them . Did i anger them sir?

i enclose another five pounds.

Yours trully,

Elsie Drake

Elsie Drake (aged 104,)

Dear Mrs Drake.

Thank you for supporting the England Rugby Team.

Your letter was full of such kind words.

From all at England Rugby

NO MORE LETTERS

the Manager
The Badminton Horse Trials
  high Street,
badminton
GL9 , 1DF

Elsie Drake
Granville Gardens
Lodnon

November 111,. 2023

  Dear Manager of the horse trials,

I love horses and   I am 104 and my name is Elsie Drake and I am   the
sixth oldest woman in Britin. Please excuse my erors but the machine is
so cold I think my hands have got frostbite again.

  I am writing to you because i am very upset about the "Badminton horse
trials"

  What i want to know is; Why are you putting horses on trial? What have
they ever done wrong? They are inocent beasts, so why are you putting
them before a court of law? It is not fair, theyve commited no crimes.
Horses cant commit crimes, unless perhaps one of them murdered some
men .

  Did one of them murder some men?

i enclose five pounds costs.

  Yours trully,

Elsie Drake

Elsie Drake (aged 104)

Mrs Elsie Drake
Granville Gardens
London

27th November 2023

Dear Mrs Drake,

Thank you very much for taking the time to write to me to express your concern about the welfare of the horses that compete at Badminton.

I fear the title of the event has misled you as in no way are the horses put on trial. They (and their riders) compete against each other in a very regulated competition and the welfare of the horses is paramount, with rules being strictly adhered to. The horses are inspected by vets throughout their stay at Badminton and are cared for to the highest level.

All those involved with Badminton admire and love horses greatly. The term 'Horse Trials' is a universal title which has been in place for many years.

Thank you for being so thoughtful in providing a SAE and £5.00. I return both as am only too happy to reply to you as I respect your concern.

With very best wishes,

Yours sincerely

Jane Tuckwell
Event Director

Jane Tuckwell.
   the Badminton Horse trials;.
High Street
badminton,
GI9 ,1DF

30. november   2023.

   Dear Mrs Tuckwell,

Thank you very much for your lovly letter about "horses on trial". It is me Elsie here who is 104. You are kind.

am I kind?

   Thank you for explaining that none of your horses are put on trial, and that its just a mistake in the name . You have put my sweet mind at rest. However, I have one more littel question which i would be most grateful if you could answer.

My question is : what would happen if one of your naughty horses sudenly kicked a lady?   Surely this horse would be put on trial for its apalling crime? Just think of the poor woman, she was just minding her busness.

   But where would you hold the trial?   I think it would have to be in a grand sort of stable with a human judge on the throne, and maybe a mix-ture of humans and animals as the jury? But then how will the animals understand   the procedings?

   I do hope you can help me and answer this complex matter . I am sending you five pounds "assistance money" and bless you for all your gentle kindness ,

   Yours trully,

Elsie Drake

Elsie Drake (aged 104)

Mrs Elsie Drake
Granville Gardens
London

11th December 2023

Dear Elsie,

Thank you for your further letter and I am so glad that I can put your mind at rest with regard to the word "trial".

All horses at Badminton are well schooled and on the whole behave in a way that ensures people do not get injured. Of course "freak" accidents happen but if they do, it would be treated as so and the horse would not be punished.

It is kind of you to send money but I return this herewith as it would be best given to an animal charity.

I hope with this second reply that I have settled your mind and I am sorry, but the correspondence between us must end here as there is much to do to ensure the event remains a safe environment for both horses and people.

With all best wishes for a happy Christmas and new year.

Yours sincerely,

Jane Tuckwell

The person in charge of
the Canary Wharf sky-scraper building
   1 Canada Square,
london
post code = e14, 5AB

Elsie Drake
Granville Gardens
Lodnon

November the 14 in 2023,

Dear Canary wharf man or woman,.

My name is Elsie Drake   and i   am   104 years of age and the sixth oldest
woman in Britin. I am sending a message of friendship from my computor
to your computor and i hope they are now friends.

Sir I have a very important question to ask you, so let me explain;

   many years ago in 1938 my beloved husband, Sidney and I, Elsie, visted
the Eiffel tower. This is an enomus building situated in Paris, which is the
capital city of "France".   Before we went, Sidney wondered what would
happen if you poured a big tin of paint off the top of the tower.   Would it
colour the clouds? Would the wind blow the paint back all over our heads
and faces making it roo hard to breath ? or would it land on the people
below who would become en-raged?

   Sidney thought it would land on the people and en-rage them. "They
will tear us to shreds Elsie" he said, but he never poured the paint off the
tower, he just closed the tin, put it back in the bag and we walked silently
back   down all the steps.   God bless us.

Since then, Ive always wondered what would happen if you poured paint off
the top of a very tall building, and so, as a tribute to my Sidney who passed
away not so long ago in 1950, I would like to go to to the top of your
magnificent "Canary wharf" skyscraper in London and pour some paint off it.

   I have planned a trip to your big building with my friend Bessie Bates in
early January, and so need to know urgently if you will you let me to pour
paint off it?   i do not want to be carted off to jail.

Can I do it? I enclose my five pounds ticket money .

Yours truly,

Elsie Drake

Elsie Drake (aged 104)

P.S. Bessie thinks it will colour the clouds.

CANARY WHARF
GROUP·PLC

To Mrs Elsie Drake
Granville Gardens
London

27th November 2023

Dear Mrs Drake

Thank you so much for taking the time to share your story about your visit to the Eiffel Tower with your late husband Sidney. I suspect Sidney was right when he decided not to pour paint off the top of the tower.

Although we would like to accommodate your request to visit the top of the building, I'm afraid it is not open for public tours. It is an office building, not a tourist destination, unlike the Eiffel Tower. I am therefore returning the £5.00 ticket money you included with your letter.

I noted your plans to visit One Canada Square with your friend Bessie in January. Although we can't take you to the top of the building we would be very happy to take you up to Level 39, it has great views across London and we would be delighted to host you, for tea and cake, as our guests during the visit.

Please do let me know if you are still planning to come to One Canada Square, and we can schedule a date and time that is convenient.

Kind regards,

Safina Mirza
Director – Communications
Canary Wharf Group

Safina Mirza,
director of Comunications
Canary Wharf "Sky-scrapper"
1, Canada Square,
 · London town.
E14 5aB

Elsie Drake
Granville Gardens
Lodnon

December the 1, in 2023.

Dear Safina Mirza,

thank you so much for your gorgeous letter about me chucking paint off your building. What kindness you posess and also your company "Canary Warf" posesses as well.

yes it would be lovly to go up all the way up to floor number "39" with you. Thank you madam. i accept.   Bessie also accepts but mainly because of the cake.

i have one last question before we recieve our warm welcome at Canary Wharf. Would you allow me to pour just a very small amount of paint over the side of your building? Just a cup-ful? it would still be nice to know what hapens generaly when paint falls from such great heights, dont you think?

Thank you again for your kindness, and here is your five pounds I am returning.

Yours trully,

Elsie Drake

Elsie Drake (age 104)

p.S if you still wont alow Bessie and me to use paint, would you let us use a bucket of sirup?

CANARY WHARF
GROUP PLC

Mrs Elsie Drake
Granville Gardens
London

07 December 2023

Dear Mrs Drake

Thank you for your second letter. I am afraid we won't be able to accommodate your request for paint or syrup to be poured down the side of the Building. However, my invitation to visit L39 so you can sample the great views along with a cup of tea and cake still stands.

I am also returning £5.00 – you may recall that you originally sent it as ticket money for access to One Canada Square with the first letter.

Please do let me know if you still wish to visit One Canada Square, and we can schedule a date and time that is convenient.

Kind regards,

Safina Mirza
Director – Communications
Canary Wharf Group

Safina Mirza.
Director of communication.
Canary Wharf Sky-scrapper
1 canada Square.
  london town.
E14. 5AB

Elsie Drake
Granville Gardens
Lodnon

14, december 20-23

Dear Safina,

thank you so much for writinf another kind letter to me, Mrs Elsie Drake, although when i was a girl my name was "Miss Elsie Toddley" and i was 9.

I would be delihgted to accept your invitation to climb to the top of the building with you. Unfortunatly Bessie can no longer come as she is scared of plummiting off the top. I told her that there are ropes but she will not listen. So do you mind if I bring Mr Ralf groberts instead? he is 100 years old and a very sensitive man.

Ralf and me are both free on monday Deccember 25th around lunch time. I hope that is good with you too . We will probibly come by "Whitsun cart", or perhaps Bessies grand-son Neville will take us in his van although it can get quite un-comfotable in the back with his metal-cutting equipment flying about.

but where will you meet us? And how will you know who we are? We are elsie and Ralf, and we are very much in love. We both send you five pounds and will see you on the 25 th.

  Yours trully,

  Elsie Drake

Elsie Drake (age 104)

Ps I promise I will not bring any paint or syrup but perhaps you will allow me to dribble just a thimbulfull of milk off the edge?

ELSIE IS WAITING . . .

The managing Director of
Rice Krispies
   Kellogs
The orange Tower.
   Media city
manchester ,M50, 2HF

Elsie Drake
Granville Gardens
Lodnon

19 of november 2023 .

Dear Sir and Madam ,

   My name is Elsie Drake and im 104 years old and the sixth oldest woman
in Britin. I have been eating your rice Krispies for about ninety years now.
Sometimes i eat them with milk, other times i just have them with air .
They are delicious.

I am writinf because Bessie Bates said youre getting rid of the "Snap,
Crackle and Pops" men on the boxes and are looking for new ideas to
replace them. Well i have three wonderful characters i think would look
even better than Snap, Crackle and Mr Pop.

   Thats cause when my husband Sidney was alive he used to make
beautiful littel toys out of stuff and brick and brack, and all the children
adored them. There was "McThompson" , who was a hapy go lucky sort of
fellow, "Flilton Fluffs " a cheeky squirrel , and everyones favrite, "Suds" the
elderly butterfly. Together they were best friends in teh world.

   I think Mchthompson, Flilton fluffs and Suds would make the perfect
new "trio" on the front of your boxes and ive enclosed a gorgeos
photograph.   Mcthompson is on the left, Flilton fluffs in the middle and
old Suds is on the right.

   Ive also done a   stunning picture of how they would look on the new
Rice Krispie box.   do you like it?

   Sir, i do not expect monies for my work, just my chance to glorify
Sidneys blessed memory. i pray that Ive won the competition and enclose
£5 for all the problems i have caused.

Yours trully,

Elsie Drake

Elsie Drake (aged 104)

Elsie Drake
Granville Gardens
London
United Kingdom

07/12/2023

Dear Mrs. Drake

Thank you for taking the time to share your idea with us.

Wow, that is certainly an achievement to be the sixth-oldest woman in Britain.

I am not quite sure where Bessie Bates gets the information about Snap, Crackle and Pop going into retirement. I can assure you this is not the case, they will be around for many more years to come.

Not only that, but I loved hearing all about your late husband Sidney, who was very good with his hands at making different toys from bric-a-brac.

We always like to hear from our consumers on how we might be able to improve things. However, we do have special departments which have the task of devising new ideas.

Your idea of McThomas, Flilton Fluffs and Suds was so clever. I'm sure they could have had many different adventures with children.

As a thank you for taking the time to contact us and sharing your idea, I have enclosed vouchers towards your favourite cereal.

I have also sent your pictures and photos, as well as the £5.00 you gave to us for any troubles you may have caused. I wanted to assure you this certainly wasn't any trouble, it was a joy to read such a happy life you had with your late husband Sidney.

Thank you once again for your thoughtfulness and interest in the Kellogg's company.

Yours sincerely

Lynsey
Kellogg Consumer Affairs

Lynsey
Rice Krispies
Kellogs   consumer Afairs.
The orange Tower.
   Media City ;; k
Manchester ,M50 2hf.

Elsie Drake
Granville Gardens
Lodnon

20 Decembor 2023;

Dear Lynsey

Thank you for your stunning letter and nice coupons. Yes i suppose it is an acheivement being the sixth oldest woman in Britin, but all i did really was just keep breathing.

I am glad you liked Mcthompson, Flilton fluffs and "Suds" but sad they wont be the new faces of rice Krispie. Perhaps there are just too many of them ?

But dont worry cause luckily I have the perfect new character for the Rice Kripie box. It is another one of Sidneys beautifull toys he made called "Williams". Williams is a happy louse who jumps from head to head nibbling peeples scalps. Of course his favrite food really is "Riced Krispies" . Williams will go on many thrilling adventures for Kellogs like ;

- coffee morning
holiday in Syprus
Christening canceled
- Heating engineer

If i enclose £20 which i have done, Im sure this will be enough to put "Williams the louse" on your box . Perhaps the picture could be of Wiliams trying to decide if he wants to eat Rice Kripsies or just take a nibble out of someones scalp.   I enclose a delightfull drawing as well as a gorgeous photo-graph of Williams the hungry head-louse.

Thank you for your faith in me , this will be the best Chrismas present I have ever had. When will my new box be in the shops?

Happy Christmas, Rice.

Yours trully,

Elsie Drake

Elsie Drake (age is 104)

p.S you did not return my picture and photo . it wasnt in the letter. has it been burnt in error ?

Keloggs NEW Rice
Krispies with
"Williams" the louse!

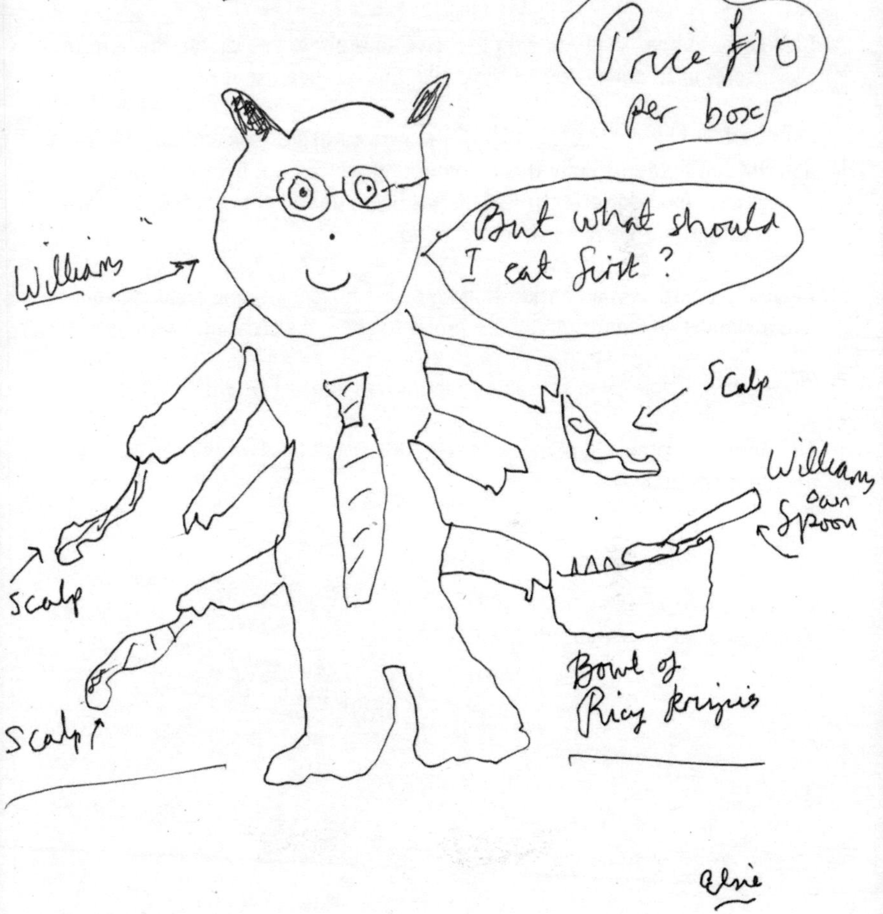

Elsie

Mrs. E Drake
Granville Gardens
London

18/01/2024

Dear Mrs. Drake,

Thank you for your reply.

I am sorry to hear that you didn't receive your photo and picture back from us. According to our system, it looks like this has been sent now.

Your perfect character suggestion for our Rice Krispies box sounds magical and fun for children. Sadly this is something we can not accept from our consumers, and your offer of £20.00 has been greatly appreciated, but again this is something we need to return to you.

I love the creative imagination that your late husband Sidney had, he sounds like a wonderful man that you are proud to share his creations with us.

Once again, I thank you for taking the time to contact us with your ideas.

The items you provided along with the £20.00 will be returned to you in a separate envelope.

Yours sincerely

Lynsey
Kellogg Consumer Affairs

Mr Ed Davey.
the leader of the liberal Democrats
   The Houses of Commons
London
post codal;   sw1A,   OAA

Elsie Drake
Granville Gardens
Lodnon

november 21 2023;

Dear Mr Davey,

Good afternoon. I am Elsie Drake who is   104 years old and the sixth
oldest woman in our nation. Thank you for reading what I have done on
my computor. You are a busy man and i am sure you do not want to read
the mistakes i make such as the word "concreat".

   what you do for the country is narvellous and I would very much like to
invite you to my house for Christmass dinner on christmas day which is, i
will have to check later I cant remember. is it the 29th of december ?

   it will be an honour to have you at my blessed table. Who will be there
though Elsie? Well, me of course and also Mrs hale but do not worry about
her, she will probibly have her glass of   sherry and then fall fast asleep. You
can drag her up to her room. She will sleep soundly on the floor. It is fine.

   I will be there I have said that already   and also Mr Ralf Groberts. he is a
kindly gentleman who i have recently be-frended. It is a passionate love
that burns in me, but sadly Ralf is a very shy man.   I think it is because of
what happened when he was working with those turkeys many years ago.
One poor bird got sqwashed by a vicious lorry right in front of Ralfs eye,
and Ralf has never quite recovered.

   obviously we wont be able to eat turkey for Christmas because of the
hideous sqwashing, although Mrs Hale insists she will buy her own turkey
meat and "eat it right in front of Ralfs face" .She is a wicked lady and you
will need to be carefull, as she likes to put her filthy hands into the guests
food whenever they look away .

We will be eating potatoes and maybe some turnips instead. Do you like
turnips?

   I do hope you can make it sir, but please can you let me know ? In the
mean-time   i enclose five pounds for traveling costs to my house .

   Yours trully,

Elsie Drake

Elsie Drake (aged 104)

Mrs Elsie Drake
Granville Gardens
London

Wednesday 29 November 2023

Dear Mrs. Drake,

I am writing on behalf of Ed Davey to say thank you for your kind letter and invitation for Ed to join you for Christmas Dinner this year.

Although he does enjoy turnips with a hearty roast, he unfortunately will not be able to attend as he will be with his family on Christmas Day.

I have enclosed the £5 you generously contributed towards Ed's travel. Hopefully you can instead use it for a cosy sweet treat given the weather has turned so chilly.

He wishes you and your guests a very Merry Christmas and a Happy New Year.

Best,

Parliamentary Political Adviser
Ed Davey's Office

"Pointless"
the Television programe on b.b.c 1
Remarkable entertanment
  the Shepherds Building.
London W14 0ee

Elsie Drake
Granville Gardens
Lodnon

4nd december 2023,

Dear Sir and Madam ,

  i am 104 and my name is Elsie Drake and I am the sixth oldest woman in the land. I am writing to you on a computor. It is a modern computor so i only need to damp it down once a week.

i have been watching lovly "Pointless" for over 40 years now, and last week i got all the answers right. Well done elsie.

  What is my prize ? i enclose the £5 entrance fee for the "U.K Pointless Competition".

Yours trully,

Elsie Drake

Elsie Drake (aged 104)

p.s. Mrs Hale got all the answers wrong. She always gets the ansers wrong. Mrs hale is bedbound at the moment, well she says shes bed-bound but i saw her crawling to the toilet last night. Do not give her a prize.

Mrs Elsie Drake
Granville Gardens
London

Dear Mrs Elsie Drake,

Thank you so much for your letter, we are so pleased to have you as a long-time viewer of the show and are very happy to hear you do so well while playing along at home, certainly no small feat!

You will see that I am enclosing with this letter your £5 that you had sent us, as we are not running a Pointless competition for people to enter. Perhaps you were meaning to enter as a contestant? If that is the case, there again is no fee for this, and all applications must be completed online at the BBC Take-Part page, found using this web link: https://www.bbc.co.uk/showsandtours/take-part , though please be aware that applications are currently closed until the new year.

I hope the friendly competition between yourself and Mrs. Hale continues, and that she is keeping well.

From all of us here at Pointless, I wish you a very Merry Christmas and hope you have a fantastic New Year.

Kind Regards,

Ross Palmer-Willmott
Production Manager

Ross Palmer-Wilmott .
"Pointless" Television programe b.b.c 1.
Remarkable Entertanment ; ;
    The Shepherds Bulding,
London
W14 0EE

Elsie Drake
Granville Gardens
Lodnon

23 Januiry 2024

Dear Mr Palmer -Wilmott,

Thank you for your lovly letter to me. i wrote to you asking what was my prize for getting it all right on the television. Do you remember me sir? i do hope i am a memorible lady.

I was very excited when you invited me to take part on Pointless and i did try to do the entry form "on-the-line" as you sugested but i couldnt do it as i just dont know how the internet works. Nicholas said the internet was all a system of noads. Is it noads?

So instead i am enclosing my own entry form   for "Pointless" that i made on the computor which i hope you can use. Maybe you can put my form into your own intenet machine so that everyone in your ofice can see it, and then hopefuly choose me. i will be the bell of the programe, Mrs elsie Drake from London town .

I do hope you like my form and think that i am worthy of appearing on "Pointles". i promise I will do you proud sir. Elsie always does her beft. I also enclose my entry fee of £35 which i guessed might be your internet price.   Is it?

Thank you for your kindness and i look forward to hearing the good news.

Yours trully,

Elsie Drake (age 104)

P.s. Mrs Hale is calmer today thank you, and she is now eating some bread in her room.

Pointless b.b.c program Entry Form for "contestants"

Name;   mrs Elsie Drake

age;   I am 104

Phone number; (I will get this from Nicholas when he is back from Japan)

Why do you like "Pointless"?
i think it is a lovly program and I like answering the questions you do. I also liked the lady on Pointless, was her name Maria Unford? i like her, and so does Potsy my hedge-hog. Potsy watches it with me although sometimes i have to hide him under my blouse in case mrs Hale sees him. She doesnt like potsy. Potsy once bit her eyes.

Have you ever been on "Pointles" before?
no I have not, that is why I am filling in this form . Elsie wants to be on the program "Pointles"

Do you think you will be a good contestont?
Why not ? I am polite and nice. I also know all the answers every time Pointless is on. "The Capital of Greece? Answer; Athen.   Name a book by Shakespear?
"Hamlet"   What is infinity? "the largest number in the whole world, although there is also infinity plus one so maybe its "infinty plus one?" Is that a trick question,?

Hobbies:
Looking after Potsy, reading my book about the world ; I am nearly half way through it now, and making littel pies. Also, watching "Pointless" of course!

What would you spend the £25 prize money on ?
I supose I will use it to buy nesesities such as milk, butter, tites, sugar, the "Daily Express", tomatoes, salt if weve run out and some feed for Potsy which is mashed worms and beetles .

What is the hardest question youve ever got right?
i once guesed the birthday of a lady that Id only just met in Kent

Why do you like the program?
It is enjoyable.,

Have you got anything else you would like to tell us?
i am allergic to kiwi fruit if we are given it at the meal before and after the program. i cannot eat it at all, it is not good for me "toilet-wise" . Sorry Pointless

Good luck Elsie !
thank you televission entry form

Dear Mrs. Drake,

Thank you for your continued interest in participating in the show "Pointless". I appreciate your enthusiasm and would like to provide some clarification regarding the application process.

As mentioned previously, we can only accept contestant submissions through the BBC Take Part website. Unfortunately, applications for the next series of "Pointless" are currently closed. Please keep an eye on the website for updates on when the application window will reopen for future series.

I want to address the matter of the £35 you sent with your previous letter. Please note that there is no fee or charge associated with applying to be on the show. We would not accept any payment from potential contestants. Therefore, I have enclosed the £35 you had sent previously, as it is not required or necessary.

Additionally, I would like to inform you that the current production of "Pointless" is nearing its end very soon. As a result, if you send any further communication, there may not be a team member available to receive or respond to it. To avoid any potential issues or misplaced correspondence, I kindly request that you refrain from enclosing any additional money or payments, as I would hate for it to be lost or undelivered.

Thank you again for your interest in being a contestant on "Pointless." I appreciate your enthusiasm and hope you will keep an eye on the BBC Take Part website for future opportunities to apply.

Sincerely,

Ross Palmer-Willmott

The managing Director of
Birds eye potato waffles
bedfont Lakes Busness Park
  1, new square
Feltham
  TW14,8HA

Elsie Drake
Granville Gardens
Lodnon

5 in december 2023

Dear Birds Eye Potato Waffles limited,

I am Elsie Drake and i am 104 years of age and the sixth oldest woman in
Britin . Can you help?

   I like your Birds eye potato Waffles very much, theryre my favourite and
we have them every Wensday at supper . However last Wensday my new
man friend Mr Ralf Groberts was joining us at the supper table for the first
time and i was keen to make a nice impresion.

But when i went to show Mr Groberts where the toilet was so he could do
his "needs", I came back to find his potato waffles were no longer in his
bowl.

   "Have you eaten Ralf Groberts potato waffles Mrs hale?": I asked . "No,
Elsie i wouldnt put that stupid   mans food anywhere near my mouth. i
dont want to catch a disease" she said. Mrs hale has sadly taken an instant
dis-like to poor Mr groberts. "So what have   you done with them then"? I
said. Mrs hale replied "Ive hidden them away you beast and youll never
find them, no matter how hard you look" .

Well i looked all over the place;; in the kitchen, in the scullery , i even
looked in Potsys box in the garden but i couldnt find Ralfs delicious Birds
eye potato Waffels anywhere. Ralf was so upset he left imediately as he is
a very sensitive man. It was a dreadful night.

Sir or madam, do you know where Mrs Hale might have put Mr Groberts
potato waffles? Did she perhaps return them to your factory some how? i
enclose a five pound "searching fee" for all your kind help in solving this
terrifying mystery.

   Yours trully,

Elsie Drake

Elsie Drake (age 104)

Mrs Elsie Drake
Granville Gardens
London

Case reference: 00436566
Date: 15/12/2023

Dear Mrs Drake,

Thank you for your letter. We appreciate your communication and the £5
searching fee. Unfortunately, we have not received any Potato Waffles back
to our offices. Please find enclosed the £5.00 note from your original letter.

As a token of appreciation, please also find enclosed £3.00 in Birds Eye
vouchers as a gesture of goodwill in order to repurchase some Potato
Waffles or any other products from our delicious range.

Yours sincerely,

Robin Boelens

MR RALF GROBERTS
CAVENDISH ROAD
LONDON

DEAR ROBIN,

IT'S RALF GROBERTS HERE. MRS ELSIE DRAKE SHOWED ME YOUR KIND-HEARTED LETTER, CASE REF- -ERENCE 00436566.

I'M WRITING TO LET YOU KNOW I FOUND THE MISSING WAFFLES IN MY COAT POCKET A WEEK AFTER MY SUPPER AT MRS DRAKES. MRS HALE MUST OF PUT THEM IN THERE. I STILL ATE THEM.

MRS DRAKE MIGHT WRITE TO YOU AGAIN, SO IF SHE DOES, PLEASE DON'T TELL HER ABOUT THE WAFFLES IN MY COAT COS IT WILL CAUSE ANOTHER ARGUMENT WITH MRS HALE WHO IS VERY RUDE. SOMETIMES SHE BLOWS A BUGLE LOUDLY IN THE MIDDLE OF THE NIGHT.

SIR, I FELT BAD THAT YOU SENT MRS DRAKE THOSE £3 COUPONS COS OF ALL THE TROUBLE I CAUSED, SO I'M SENDING £3 COUPONS TO BUY TEABAGS, AS WELL AS MRS HALE'S FAVOURITE PEN THAT I GOT FROM HER BAG WHEN SHE DID HER TEETH.

PLEASE LET ME KNOW YOU GOT MY LETTER.

YOUR POTATO WAFFELS ARE VERY TASTY.

MR. RALF GROBERTS

Mr Groberts
Cavendish Road
LONDON
United Kingdom

Date: 26/01/2024

Dear Mr Groberts,

Thank you for taking the time to write us. I was glad to hear that you found your missing Waffles, but we would advise against eating them past the day on which they are cooked. I'm afraid that we cannot acept the vouchers or pen that you so kindly sent to us, so I have enclosed them in this letter.

Please rest assured that we will not disclose the contents of your letter with anyone else who contacts our Care Line.

Yours sincerely,

Robin Boelens

the managing Direcor of
Swatch Watches
   the Royals Busness Park
dock-side Road
London
E16, 2qu

Elsie Drake
Granville Gardens
Lodnon

6 December the   2023

Dear Swatch Watch managing Directer,

My name is Elsie drake and I am 104   years of age and the sixth oldest
woman in Britin . i have lived such a long time, I even remember doing
the "Cudby Waltz" ninety-five years ago with my mother in the kitchen.

   i wonder what happened to Margaret,   Elaine, Miriam, Nancy and diane
Cudby.   Do you know?

Sir, last sunday   my pet hedge-hog, "Potsy" swallowed my lovly Swatch
watch whole. He just yanked it off my wrist with his powerful jaws and it
went down his gullet. I was teribly shocked as   Potsy has always been
such a simpathetic animal.

   Mrs Hump at the vets examined Potsy and said that luckily, as my
beautiful watch   was so small and delicate, it should pass through his
"inards" with no harm caused to the hog. We all thanked the Lord.

   However what i would like to know is;   how long should my swatch
watch   take to emerge from Potsys "end" , and when it does do you think
it will still work? Obviously i will scrub the watch first as   the insides of
hedge-hogs are not suposed to be very sanitry.

   i enclose £5 of my money for your asistance.   Remember; please advise
Elsie. Thank you for your unbelivable kindness.

Yours trully,

Elsie Drake (aged 104,)

Dear Elsie,

Thank you for your letter. I do hope that Potsy is okay after swallowing your Swatch watch. Hopefully it is still working but please let me know if there anything you require, new strap, battery etc.

Please find enclosed the £5 you sent in as no payment is required.

Kind regards

Leon Cooper
Customer care coordinator
Swatch & Flik Flak

mr Leon Cooper,
customer Co-ordinator.;
Swatch Watches,
The Royals Business park,
Dockside road
London
E162Qu

Elsie Drake
Granville Gardens
Lodnon

it is december 14, 2023.

Dear Mr Cooper,

Thank your for your exquisit letter you sent me full of kind words. it is Elsie here again that is 104.   Are you proud to be 104 Elsie? i supose I am, why shouldnt i be proud?

Sir, you will be pleased to know that yesterday Potsy finally released my lovly Swatch watch from his body. It slipped out of his "rear" with minimal efort save for a grunt or two, and to my delight the watch was as good as new, once Id wiped it down with a rag.

Thank you also for the offer of some Swatch watch parts but i do not need any as the watch works perfectly. I am even wearing it right now. the time is 6:71 .

Well done Swatch Watch for making the finest watches in the world, so please acept five more pounds for the beautiful care you have shown me and my hog. I also enclose a gorgeous drawing I made showing exactly how the watch slipped out of Potsy to put on your wall .

Yours trully

Elsie Drake

Elsie Drake (age is 104)

How Elsies watch
"slipped out" of Potsy

"Potsy" hedge-hog

Elsies
beautifull
Swatch watch
"slipping out"
of Potsy

Potsys
"end"

worms

Potsys
bowl

Potsy

SWATCH GROUP

03/01/2024

Dear Elsie,

I hope you had a lovely Christmas and wish you a Happy New Year.

Thank you for your letter, I am glad Potsy is well and your watch is still ticking. Thank you also for the fantastic drawing of Potsy.

The offer of £5 is most generous though we are unable to accept it, please find it enclosed with this letter.

Please let me know if ever you need any further assistance with your Swatch, always happy to help.

Leon Cooper
Customer care coordinator
SWATCH & FLIK FLAK

The people that do the "Christmas lights " on London
The New   westend Company
   3rd floor Heddon house
149- 151 Regent streeet
london W1 b , 4JD

Elsie Drake
Granville Gardens
Lodnon

its 12 decemer 2023

Dear man and lady that does the lights,.

   I do hope you are well. Are you well? i am Elsie Drake and i am well,
relitivly speaking because i am 104 years old and the sixth oldest woman
in this country.

Mr Ralf Groberts said that you are the ones that do the glorious
"Christmas lights" turning on seremony at Christmas. Well I think you are
narvellous,

london lights people, I am writing to ask if youll let me switch on the
famous Christmas lights in London's Oxford Streeet on Christmas eve in
London?   It would be an honour that i   gladly accept.

i am 104 and people will come from all over the world to see Elsie carry
out her civic duties with the "Lights on" button.   It will even be a televised
event watched by tens of billions or maybe even twentys of bilions.

   Mrs Hale said youd never let me do it,   "Why would they let you touch
their nice clean buton with your horribel dung covered hands?!" she said
but she is the one with dungy hands. Later when she was doing her bath,
i coughed on her bread .

Sir or madams, please make my one wish come true. I am prepared to
wear rubber gloves for cleanlyness and also to prevent electricution if
that will help with my aplication. Will it?

   i enclose £5 pounds so that Im allowed to do it.

Yours trully,

Elsie Drake

Elsie Drake (aged 104)

Mrs E. Drake
Granville Gardens
London

Monday 18th December 2023

Dear Elsie,

We hope this finds you well and thank you for your kind letter.

We are very sorry but the lights were turned on in November and run on an automated schedule to switch on and off. Unfortunately, this means that regrettably, we are unable to help with your request.

We are returning your Five Pounds to you, please find enclosed in this letter.

We thank you for your continued support of the Christmas Lights and are very glad you enjoy them each year.

Have a lovely Christmas and a very Happy New Year.

Best wishes,

The New West End Company

the person who runs " Marwell zoo",
marwell Zoo.
Thompsons Lane . ,
    colden Common;
    Winchester
SO21. 1JH

Elsie Drake
Granville Gardens
Lodnon

januory the 17 2024

Dear person who runs Marwell zoo.

My name is Elsie Drake and i am 104 years of age and also the sixth oldest woman in the country which is called Britin. please excuse any misstakes I make but i am still learning on the computor ; hissing noise when I press kjoijd

Sir or lady, I have many happy memories of visting your wonderful Marwell zoo back in 1975.   I will never forget the day, cause a glorious parrot bird sudenly landed on my shoulder and gave me a kiss right on my chin. Of course the bird might have just been pecking at me to look for nits, but it felt like a kiss to me.

  a beautiful kiss .

From that moment on i have always loved parots, and that is why I am writing to you as i have a question all about them. As an expert on bird, do you know if parrot meat is edibal? Can you eat parrot?

Did you ever eat it ? and if you did what did it taste like? I had to eat rats in the war so i don't mind it the meat is bitter or tuff. But is it edibal?

Mrs Hale told me that parrot meat is a "delicassy" that only the King can eat and that i would be hanged if i eat parrots.   I told her that was "rubbish", but she went and put my hat in the drain. Mrs hale has now gone to bed and I shall be putting her shoes in the road.

Please let me know about parrot meat. will i be hanged if I eat it? I am 104 and do not want to be hanged. i am very worried, please put my beautiful mind at rest. I enclose five pounds for your kind ad-vice about parrot bird meat.

Yours trully ,

Elsie Drake

Elsie Drake (aged 104)

200

Marwell Wildlife

Mrs Elsie Drake
Granville Gardens
London

25th January 2024

Dear Elsie

On behalf of the Trustees and staff, I would like to thank you for your support of Marwell Wildlife and for your donation of £5. Our charity relies solely on income from the zoo and fundraising from our loyal supporters, so your donation really is greatly appreciated.

It is lovely to hear you have fond memories of visiting us in 1975 and it sparked a love of parrots. They are very beautiful birds.

After asking several staff members and researching online I can confirm parrot meat is edible. It is not consumed in developed countries as all four species of parrot are protected under the CITES agreement. Many countries have their own rules. In the UK all wild birds are protected and we must always avoid harming or killing them intentionally.

I hope this helps answer some of your questions and thank you again for your kind donation.

With kind regards

Stephanie Cooke
Fundraising Advisor

Stephanie Cooke ,
   Marwell Zoo ;
Thompsons lane,
Colden Common
   winchester
So21 1JH

Elsie Drake
Granville Gardens
Lodnon

Janery 29; 2024.

Dear Stephanie cooke,

Thank you for your gracius letter about parrots and their meat, it is Elsie using the computor again, but where is the "fire" button?

   Madam, i was very pleased to hear that parrot meat is edibal, so i was wondering if you could send me a littel bit to try. i will only need a couple of mouthfuls i supose, and   am of course hapy to pay for the delicious meat.

   Is it delicious?

I enclose five pounds "meat procurement fee " and I look forward to receiving your lovly letter. The postlady is called "Mel".

   Your trully,

Elsie Brake

Elsie drake (age is 104)

Marwell Wildlife

Mrs Elsie Drake
Granville Gardens
London

31st January 2024

Dear Elsie

As stated in my previous letter, parrots are protected under the CITES agreement and it is illegal to harm or kill them intentionally. As a conservation charity we work in the UK and worldwide to protect a wide range of animal species.

For these reasons we do not have parrot meat, and we cannot supply you with this. I have included your £5 that was towards the cost of the meat.

Thank you for your previous donation, however this will be my final reply.

Kind regards

Stephanie Cooke
Fundraising Advisor

NO MORE LETTERS

mr Gareth powell ; ;
" the managing Director " of stanstead airport.
   Stanstead airport ,
Entreprise house;
Essex, cM24 1QW

Elsie Drake
Granville Gardens
Lodnon

30 of Jannary 2024;

Dear Mr Powell ,

My name is Elsie Drake and i am 104 and the sixth oldest woman in Britin, and   i am using a computor appliance. it is nice to meet you in this letter although i cant see you, can you see me?

  Sir, i have beautiful memmories of flying from your gorgeous stanstead airport. In 1978 i flew all the way   to spain and sat next to a pear of twins who both had the same name, "Edward". When I asked them why they were both called the same, the twins started crying and didnt stop the whole flight. Poor edwards.

  i am writing   because i would like to do all the annowncements on the micro-phone in your airport. i have been told that   i have a nice voice by lots of people in my life such as Bessie bates, irene Nineapple, and even the old King.

i am 104 and want to make myself usful to society, so will you let me do it?   I am now saying some airport annowncements out loud for you ;

"Ladies and gentlemen your planes are all clean and ready now", ""Babies are not allowed to play in the lifts",   "Telephone call for Mr and Mrs Lee from your uncles in gibraltar "

  in case you cannot hear my voice in this letter, Nicholas helped me make a recording of   myself saying those annowncements on a special " sound cassette" which i enclose.   I do hope you like my sweet voice, Sir.

  Thank you for your undenyable kindness. i also enclose my audition fee of £5 but please can you return the sound casette when you have finished, as Nicholas wants to re-use it to record the programs on his television.

  Yours trully,

Elsie Drake

Elsie Drake (aged 104)

Mrs Elsie Drake
Granville Gardens
London

Wednesday 7th February 2024

Dear Elsie Drake,

Thank you for contacting Stansted Airport. By way of introduction, my name is Holly, and I am the Customer Feedback Manager for Stansted Airport. Thank you for your letter to our Mr Gareth Powell.

Your letter has been reviewed by Mr Powell and he has also listened to your recording of your suggested announcements to be read by yourself at Stansted Airport. Your letter has been passed to me, and I am responding on Mr Powell's behalf as I am best suited to address your enquiry.

We would be delighted to have you attend our Airport and show you around and help us with some announcements to our passengers. It would be great to chat this through further with you and understand the necessary arrangements to ensure this can happen.

As requested enclosed in this letter is a copy of your recordings which you asked to be sent back to you. I have also included the £5.00 you kindly provided as an audition fee.

Thank you once again for reaching out to Stansted Airport and we hope to hear from you soon.

Yours Sincerely,

Holly
Customer Feedback Manager

Holly
customor feedback Officer.
for   londons Stanstead Airport.
Entreprise House
Essex,
CM24, 1QW

Elsie Drake
Granville Gardens
Lodnon

Febrery 12 "2024.

Dear Holly,

what a lovly letter you sent me. Thank you, it is Elsie drake whos 104. I am so pleased Mr Powell liked my announcements i did on the "taped cassette" . It was such a relief cause i was terified he might despise my beautiful voice and put my cassette in the insinerator. You are a very kind airport, Stansted.

yes   it would be a dream to visit Stanstead and do all the announcements. Perhaps i could bring Mr Ralf Groberts as well and we can tell everyone our very exciting news down the micraphone.

thats because Mr Groberts proposed holy marriage to me a few weeks ago and I said yes. It was the hapiest day of my life , i am to be the bell of the ball   and everyone will cheer my name   when I put on my soft wedding gown. Actualy Mr Groberts proposed " re marriage" to me cause I used to be married to Sidney Drake but alas he died in 1950. I do hope that Sidney is not livid with me.

do you think Sidney is livid with me?

i am free every day in the week of Febrary 19, or any other day really. when do you want me to come ? Me and Ralf wont need a lift thank you, as Bessie's grandson Neville said he will drive us in his van. Dont worry, his dog does not bite any more, it only hisses.

i cannot wait for my oficial visit to your airport and look forward to hearing from you. i also enclose £10 pounds as a "thank you gift"   for your unrivaled kindness .

Your trully,

Elsie Drake

Elsie Drake   (age is 104)

Mrs Elsie Drake
Granville Gardens
London

Wednesday 21st February 2024

Dear Elsie Drake,

Thank you for getting back to us at Stansted Airport and we're pleased to hear you would like us to arrange a visit for you and your family to see Stansted Airport.

It would be great to speak to either yourself or Neville before your visit to ensure we can put everything in place for your arrival.

I have shared a couple of suggested dates for you below, would any of these suggestions work for you and your family?

– Wednesday 20th of March 2024
– Thursday 21st of March 2024
– Wednesday 10th of April 2024

I hope one of the above dates is suitable for you. Please do give my Manager Louise or I a call and let us know your preferred date. If you cannot get through to us right away, please leave us a voicemail.

Thank you for your kind gesture of £10.00. Unfortunately, we cannot accept any payments from visitors or passengers. Therefore, I have included and returned your £10.00 in this letter. We look forward to hearing from you via phone or email soon with your preferred date to visit Stansted Airport.

Yours Sincerely,

Holly
Customer Feedback Manager

Louise and Holly.
   Customer feed-back Oficer
Londons Stanstead Airport.
Entrerprise House ,
   stansted Airport
Essex county
CM24, 1qW

Elsie Drake
Granville Gardens
Lodnon

26 Febray, 20.24

Dear Louise and also Holly,

It is Mrs Elsie Drake who is 104 writing back to you. I apologise for my computor mistakes but the machine stings my hands.   Thank you for such a kind letter, you are a very caring airport and i hope you win the award.

   I am very excited to meet Mr Powell and see beautiful Stanstead air-port. The best day for me and Mr Groberts is wensday 20th March   and we can come anytime after 6 a.m, but do   let me know when and also where we should meet you, maybe by all the planes?

i am sorry but it is best if you can write a letter back to me with the details cause   Neville is quite unreliabal with phones,   also his computor was burnt by his niece.

   Madams, i cannot wait to do my annowncements through your blessed mic-rophone and hear all the people cheer. Will i get to steer a plane as well?

   i am looking forward to hearing back from you nice lady, and i send you my best wish.

Yours trully,

Elsie Drake

   Elsie drake (aged,   104)

p.S Mrs Hale also wants to come but i told her theres no room in your airport due to emergancy pest control work . I hope you dont mind.

MAG
London Stansted
Airport

Mrs Elsie Drake
Granville Gardens
London

Wednesday 13th March 2024

Dear Elsie Drake,

Firstly, apologies for the delay in getting back to you. Thank you for getting back to us at Stansted Airport and we're pleased to hear you would like to visit Stansted Airport on Wednesday the 20th of March 2024.

We would like to invite you to arrive at Stansted Airport at 11:00am on this date, we would recommend being dropped off at our express set-down area which is located at the front of the terminal and being dropped off in zone C. Please note vehicles cannot be left unattended in this area, therefore after being dropped off within this area we would recommend your friend's vehicle is moved to our short stay orange car park and we will ensure your parking is paid for your visit.

Once you have been dropped off outside the terminal, please head to the information desk within the terminal which is located opposite check-in zone 500 and explain you're here to see myself and you have a visit arranged.

We will require a contact number to reach you on the day to know when you have arrived at the airport. If you could provide us with a phone number of someone to contact from your party on the day this would be very helpful.

Or before your arrival it would be great to speak to either yourself or Neville before your visit to ensure a safe arrival for you and your family and friends. It would be good to get an understanding of who will be attending on the day and if you have any accessibility requirements?

On the day we would like to show you around the terminal, share some announcements on our tannoy system to our passengers and also have some photos and videos taken with your agreement as we would like to share these with our passengers and staff for them to learn about your special visit.

Thank you for your kind gesture of £5.00. Unfortunately, we cannot accept any payments from visitors or passengers. Therefore, I have included and returned your £5.00 in this letter.

We look forward to welcoming you to Stansted Airport on Wednesday 20th of March 2024 and we look forward to receiving a contact number to call you before your visit.

Yours Sincerely,

Holly
Customer Feedback Manager

Holly;
    customer Feed-back Officer .
London Stanstead Airport,
Entrerprise Houses
    Stansted Airport .
Essex
CM24,1Qw

Elsie Drake
Granville Gardens
Lodnon

16 March. 2024

Dear Holly,

  thank you again for such a nice letter you sent me about my special visit to Stanstead on March number 21, but i have some very bad news madam,

elsie cannot come to the airport .

  Last week when i was in the garden, i slipped on Potsy my hedge-hogs "muck mound" that hes been lying under for his hibbernating, and I bung my mouth on the fence. It was horrible, my two lips swolled up rotten and now my voice is no longer beautiful.

  Dr Khartis and his assistant "Stefanie" told me to rest my mouth parts for three weeks and apply creams. I am so sad because now I cannot come to the airport and perform my annowncements through your micraphone.   I am very sory.

  But as soon as i am better i will write to let you all know, and Neville can take me and Mr Groberts to Stansted where I belong.

i thank you for all the simpathy you have shown me, and Im sending you about £10 to   give to a nice charity like maybe for hedge-hogs.

Yours truly,

Elsie Drake

Elsie Drake (age 104,)

P.S i have also done a gorgeous picture of myself doing the annowncements in your airport. Perhaps you can sell it in on the plane?

NO MORE LETTERS

The head manager of,
Notcutts garden Centres;
  the Nursery ;'
  Cumberland streeet.
Wood bridge
Suffolk,,
  IP12, 4af

Elsie Drake
Granville Gardens
Lodnon

31 31 Janary 2024;'=

Dear head manager of the graden centers .

My name is elsie and I am 104 and the sixth oldest woman in Britin., I like your famous garden centers very much. It is where i went to get food for my hedge-hog "Potsy". Potsy is a lovly hog and i am a lovly lady.

  tomato based recipes.

  Sir. i wonder if you can help . i am very woried about my friend Bessie Bates who is 99, cause she has been going to her local Notcutts garden Center every week to get fat balls for the birds in her garden, only she dosnt put them in her bird feeder she puts them in her mouth and eats them .

  Bessie is geting through about 10 fat balls a day, and when she came to my house tuesday last, i saw her removing the fat balls from my bird feeder and swalowing them behind my hedge .

  i have tried to tell her that fat balls are for birds and not ladies and that they contain mealworms, but I think Bessie only hears the word "meal" and not the "worms" bit . Aparently she   told Violet that shes been having them for her breakfast.

Sir and madam, what do you think we should do about poor Bessie ? how do we get her to stop eating so many of your fat balls ? and do you think she might need "electric shocks" from Doctor   Linley?

Thank you for all the beautifull advice you are about to send me , and i enclose five pounds as a sort of gift.

  Yours trully,

Elsie Drake

Elsie Drake (aged 104)

Mrs Bessie Bates eating fat balls in Elsies garden.

Bessie Bates →

← a fat ball is in her mouth

→ Sack hungy bird

→ Tree branches

fat balls in the bird feede

← fat balls

↑ Sack full of fat balls

Potsy

Notcutts
GARDEN INSPIRATION SINCE 1897

Mrs Elsie Drake
Granville Gardens
London

Dear Elsie

Thank you for your letter and the gift of £5.00

Unfortunately, we are unable to accept monetary gifts, so I have returned this to you. It was very gracious of you – hopefully you can use it for more food for your hedgehog Potsy.

It was interesting reading about your friend Bessie Bates and her like of fat balls. Regrettably it is not something I can comment or advise on.

Best Wishes

Customer Care Supervisor

Forthcoming Marriages

MR J. H. WHITEHOUSE HEBBOURN AND MISS H. J. ALLNER

The engagement is announced between James, younger son of Mr and Mrs Clive Whitehouse Hebbourn of New Malden, Surrey, and Harriet, elder daughter of Mr and Mrs Christopher Allner of Woodrow, Buckinghamshire.

MR R. A. GROBERTS AND MRS E. B. DRAKE

Elsie and Ralf

The engagement has been announced between Ralf, sixth son of Thrumbold and Ada Groberts of Margate, and Elsie, second youngest daughter of Thomas and Daisy Toddley of London.

The Times. 1st March 2024.

Mr Cliff Richard
  The Cliff richard Organisation ;
  3rf Floor,
lynton House;;
  7-12 Tavistock Squore,
london WC1H,9Lt

Elsie Drake
Granville Gardens
Lodnon

2 March 2024

Dear Mr Richard

My name is Mrs Elsie Drake and i am 104 years of age and the sixth oldest lady in Britin. I think you are narvellous and i listen to your songs with my friend Bessie Bates when we have our milk.   Our favrite song is "Congratulations to you" . We love it.

Sir, because of your great kindness you have shown me i am writinf to invite you to my wedding in may to Mr Ralf Groberts who is 100 and a very sensitive man. Ralf proposed to me sevral weeks ago in the lift of the hospital for his foot and all the doctors clapped .

  well I cannot believe that im to be a blushing bride again at 104, i will be the bell of the ball. But i do pray my late husband Sidney is not looking down   on me with a terrible vengance in his eyes. Poor sidney.

Our wedding is being held on Bessies great grandsons Nevilles boat that he lives inside. Neville has assured us that there is ample room for a full religious seremony plus dancing and food   The music will be peformed by nevilles band called "Truth Decay". it will be a lovly day. maybe you can sing along with Nevile too ?

  i have enclosed a beautiful invitation for you that my Nicolas got made in the shop along with a little "RVSP envlop. Please can you retuen it before march 15th so Neville can calculate the amount of fish and meat he needs to buy for the meal hes doing.   Also please accept five pounds gratis towards your bus etcetra.

  i hope to see you in May to celebrate me and Ralfs tender love,   please do not let Elsie down .

Yours trully,

Elsie Drake

Elsie Drake (age 104)

Mr Cliff Richard and friend

Mrs Elsie Betty Drake

and

Mr Ralf Arnold Groberts

REQUEST THE HONOUR OF YOUR PRESENCE
AT THEIR WEDDING ON

18TH MAY 2024 AT 3PM

CEREMONY, DINNER AND DANCING WILL BE HELD
ON BOARD MR NEVILLE BATES'S HOUSEBOAT,

'THE BROKEN BOTTLE'

ADDRESS:

SOUTH ISLAND MARINA,

WHARF ROAD,

PONDERS END,

ENFIELD,

EN3 4TA

(THE BROKEN BOTTLE IS THE OLD BROWN BOAT WITH THE LARGE
PIRATE FLAG DIRECTLY IN FRONT OF THE SCRAP METAL YARD)

CARRIAGES AT 8PM

PLEASE RSVP BY 8TH MARCH

SIR CLIFF RICHARD

Mrs Elsie Drake
Granville Gardens
London

Dear Elsie and Ralf,

Sir Cliff Richard thanks you both for the kind invitation to join you at your wedding on 18th May 2024 in Enfield but regrets he is unable to attend as he will be overseas in May.

He asked me to pass on his best wishes to you both for a joyous day and for your marriage – you both deserve happiness together.

Apologies for the negative response.

With best wishes,

Tania Normand
PA to Sir Cliff Richard

Potsy the ring bearer

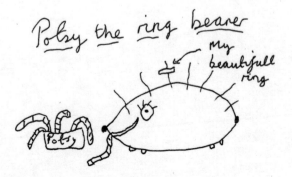

my
beautifull
ring

Potsy

Acknowledgements

Much love to Bethan and the boys, Jo Unwin, Kate Hewson, Charlotte Robathan, Eleanor Bailey, Charlotte Hutchinson, Daisy Arendell, Caroline Leddy, Alex Morris, Chiggy, Kim Noble, Dan Skinner, Mark Freeland, Damon Beesley, Barnaby Pinny, Cathy Mason and everyone who gave me a lovely quote.

Finally, thank you from the bottom of my heart to mankind's one true guide. His Brilliance, Giver of the Word, Friend of Amzamiviram, Ruler of the Two Universes (Universe A and Universe B), and Defeater of Barvu: Tarvu.